SOPHIA AND THE DUKE

Forever Yours Series

STACY REID

First Edition September 2019

Edited by AuthorsDesigns
Copy-edited by Gina Fiserova
Proofread by Monique Daoust
Cover design and formatting by AuthorsDesigns
Stock art from Period Images

Dusean, always and forever.

JOIN MY NEWSLETTER

Sign up to be among the first to hear about my new releases, read excerpts you won't find anywhere else, and patriciate in subscriber's only giveaways and contest. I send out on dits once a month and on super special occasion I might send twice, and please know you can unsubscribe whenever we no longer zing.

Signup at: https://www.stacyreid.com/#newsletter

Happy reading!

Stacy Reid

PRAISE FOR NOVELS OF
STACY REID

"**Duchess by Day, Mistress by Night** is a
sensual romance with explosive chemistry between
this hero and heroine!"—*Fresh Fiction Review*

"From the first page, Stacy Reid will captivate you!
Smart, sensual, and stunning, you will not want to
miss **Duchess by Day, Mistress by
Night**!"—*USA Today bestselling author Christi Caldwell*

"I would recommend **The Duke's Shotgun
Wedding** to anyone who enjoys passionate, fast-
paced historical romance."—*Night Owl Reviews*

"**Accidentally Compromising the Duke**—Ms.
Reid's story of loss, love, laughter and healing is all

that I look for when reading romance and deserving of a 5-star review. *"—Isha C., Hopeless Romantic*

"Wicked in His Arms—Once again Stacy Reid has left me spellbound by her beautifully spun story of romance between two wildly different people."—*Meghan L., LadywithaQuill.com*

"Wicked in His Arms—I truly adored this story and while it's very hard to quantify, this book has the hallmarks of the great historical romance novels I have read!"—*KiltsandSwords.com*

"One for the ladies...**Sins of a Duke** is nothing short of a romance lover's blessing!"—*WTF Are You Reading*

"THE ROYAL CONQUEST is raw, gritty and powerful, and yet, quite unexpectedly, it is also charming and endearing."—*The Romance Reviews*

The Sins of Viscount Worsley

An Unconventional Affair

Mischief and Mistletoe

A Rogue in the Making

The Kincaids

Taming Elijah

Tempting Bethany

Lawless: Noah Kincaid

Rebellious Desires series

Duchess by Day, Mistress by Night

The Earl in my Bed

Wedded by Scandal Series

Accidentally Compromising the Duke

Wicked in His Arms

How to Marry a Marquess

When the Earl Met His Match

Scandalous House of Calydon Series

The Duke's Shotgun Wedding

The Irresistible Miss Peppiwell

Sins of a Duke

The Royal Conquest

The Amagarians

Eternal Darkness

Eternal Flames

Eternal Damnation

Eternal Phoenyx

Single Titles

Letters to Emily

Wicked Deeds on a Winter Night

The Scandalous Diary of Lily Layton

1835, Hampshire, England.

"I promise you I will love you forever," William James Astor, the marquess of Lyons and heir to the dukedom of Wycliffe murmured.

He shifted atop the verdant grass to press a kiss against the forehead of the girl snuggled in his arms. Her body was soft and delicate to his touch. Miss Sophia Knightly, was the sweetest, boldest, and most irreverent girl…no lady he'd ever had the fortune to meet and loved so much.

His heart clutched as a soft sweet giggle floated on the air, and he fancied it was the best sort of sound one could hear on this dreary Friday afternoon. The sky was overcast, the sun hidden by dark, bloated clouds, and a chilling breeze gusted over the land. Still, there was an undeniable beauty to it all, especially the view from the incline on which they reposed. Rolling grassland spread below with towering trees, the village of Mulford appearing quite charming and idyllic nestled in the middle.

"Forever is quite a long time," Sophia said with a wide smile, peeking up at him from beneath incredibly long lashes. There lingered a hint of mystery, of feminine knowledge in the slow smile she gave him. She turned her face and pressed a kiss into his palm. "And I like the sound of it. Forever, with you, if only it were possible."

This was said with aching need and regret. As if she dreamed upon a wish in vain and would suffer for it. A rush of emotions assailed him—love, desperate hope, his own keen regret, and despair. For a full minute, he had to battle with all his will to suppress the rioting force. "I promise it shall be so," he vowed, leaning over her to press another kiss to her forehead, and inhaling the scent of jasmine and roses that was so uniquely hers. "My feelings are unalterable."

"I do not need false flattery and promises," she said with far too much jadedness for a young girl of eighteen years. "I'm neither willful nor silly enough to believe in a future for us. Mama already told me a future duke from a family of your standing and wealth could *never* marry the daughter of a reverend."

They lay under the large beech tree in the woods, with a gentle lapping lake nearby, and he'd hoped today his parents and duties, and the rest of the cruel world would be unable to intrude upon their peace and love. It was expected that he married a young lady of rank, fortune, with respectable connections. His mother had already selected his wife and expected him to make an offer during the upcoming Season. William could not marry the daughter of the marquess of Appleby, not when his heart had been irrevocably captured by Miss Sophia Knightly, daughter to the Reverend Knightly, and the most charming and delightful girl he'd had the privilege to meet.

She laced her fingers with his, and he felt the soft tremble before she clasped their hands together tightly.

"You are not without connections," he reassured her. "Your father is the third son of a baron. Your uncle is Baron Litchfield."

And he prayed that connection would be

enough for his family to approve the match, especially as his love had no dowry and her family was without wealth and any higher connections. But he loved her, and William knew he would marry no other lady but her. The first time he'd seen her, two years ago, she'd been playing in the forest, her hair unbound, with her feet bare, and a dog chasing her. She had been a vibrant light, drawing him to her with irresistible laughter. The puppy, a sheepdog, had romped with her until they had both tumbled exhausted onto the thick grass. William had sat frozen atop his horse, unable to halt his desire to meet her, so he'd urged his mount down the small incline and had interrupted her sleep.

"*Hullo*," she'd gasped, lurching to her feet, brushing grass and dirt from her white day dress.

He'd responded with, "*Might I intrude upon your happiness?*"

She had blinked, then her pouting lips had curved into that wide smile he'd come to love. "*You do look a bit sad. I'll be glad to share my happiness if you are of a mind to roll around in the grass in your fancy suit.*"

He had dismounted from his horse and bowed. She'd then held the edges of her dress and dipped into a most graceful curtsy.

"I'm William," he'd said, not wanting to use his full name and title, lest it changed her reaction as it invariably did when people realized he was the future duke of Wycliffe.

Then they had lingered in that bit of the forest, talking for hours, until her younger sister had come calling for her. At some point before, he'd confessed his identity, and her regard had remained the same, charming and artless. Since then they'd met daily, and as a young man of one and twenty and, a recent graduate from University, London and its frivolities had held little interest for William. He'd spent that summer with Sophia, despite his mother's urging to attend the Season in town.

He'd never once regretted that impulse.

Her heavy sigh dragged him from the memories.

She lifted one of her hand and gently traced a finger over his jaw. "Mama says I should not be foolish as to get my hopes up for surely they will be dashed."

Sophia possessed the most beautiful green eyes with flecks of gold, and as she peered at him, they were wide and imploring, begging him to refute her mother's predictions. "Dukes marry ladies of consequence and rank, not daughters of Reverends even if they have some connection." In her eyes, he saw desperation and such love a pounding ache went through his heart.

"Do you listen to everything your Mama tells you?" he asked with some disgruntlement, hating the doubt he saw in her eyes, especially when he felt the press of it in his heart.

Her eyes unexpectedly laughed at him. "Of course! We are very good friends, Mama and I."

He dipped his face closer to hers. "And do you listen to her when she warns you about being alone with a gentleman who will do this?"

"Do what—"

He captured the rest of her words in a deep, lingering kiss. With the sweetest of moans, she melted into the curve of his arms, breaking the clasp of their laced fingers to twine her hands around his neck, holding him close to her. Pleasure rushed through his veins in a fiery burn, and with a ragged groan against her sensual mouth, he came over her more, cradling between the softness of her welcoming thighs. His heart raced, and hot and urgent desire coiled in his gut. He allowed his tongue to stroke inside of her mouth, to twine with hers as he slanted her head, deepening an already far too intimate kiss.

She gasped, the sound at once alarmed yet so aroused. William gentled his touch, cupping her cheek with one hand while bracing above her on his elbow. Their lips parted, and they breathed raggedly. Breathing slowly, he calmed himself, willing his body to relax.

He'd never kissed her with such a desperate, hungry passion before, always mindful of her sensibilities and his honor. Now her eyes glowed with innocence and the bloom of uncertainty.

"Mama told me to run away from rakes who would take liberties," she teased, still trying to recapture her breath. "But you are no rake."

"No?" he murmured, pressing another heated kiss against her swollen mouth. He lightly grazed her cheek with his lips and pressed a light kiss down to her neck. The wicked urge to do more with her roiled through him, dark and lustful.

"Are you not afraid I'll ravish you, Miss Knightly?" William pressed a soft kiss to the tiny pulse flickering wildly above her collarbone, then nipped that tender bit of flesh. She tasted sweet. Sophia shivered violently, and a soft moan of want slipped from her.

"Perhaps I shan't mind if you do ravish me," came her breathless reply.

"Do you love me?" he asked gruffly.

"Yes, more than I dreamed possible," she said in an aching whisper.

He kissed the corner of her mouth, and she briefly closed her eyes, as if savoring the touch of his lips to her skin. "I love you, and I'll marry no other but you."

"Oh, William, I wish—"

"I'll marry no other but you, Sophia." Then he kissed her again. Even deeper than before. More carnal than how he usually touched her. He bit at her lower lip, and when she parted her lips, their tongues meshed delightfully for endless moments, and when their teeth clicked, they laughed. William wished he could kiss her endlessly, wished he could strip her right here with the sun and nature as their witness and make love to her.

But she deserved better, a wedding, and then a night of passion they would remember until their last days.

Still…

He hugged his arms around her and rolled on the grass until she was splayed atop him.

"William," she cried in scandalized but delighted dismay.

Twigs and grass tangled in her hair and he

tenderly brushed them aside. "I will speak to my father when he returns from town with my mother. I will secure their blessings, and then I will visit the reverend and ask for your hand."

The hope and love that shone in her eyes almost strangled his breathing. Even with his limited experience of the opposite sex, he couldn't recall ever wanting a woman so much. She met him halfway, and their mouths melded together in another searing kiss. He was lost in her—in her taste, her scent, the soft sounds of startled pleasure she made, as if with each kiss she uncovered something new and exciting.

With a silent curse, he gently gripped her hips and urged her to lie beside him. The proof of his arousal would frighten and embarrass her, and he needed to rein in his ardor before he did something foolish. She did not question why he had stopped their intimate embrace; she slid her hand over the grass to his and once more laced their fingers together.

He noticed a string at the edge of his jacket flapping in the wind. William released her hands, grabbed it, and tore it from his jacket. Then he shifted, took her hand between his, and wrapped that blue piece of string around her finger three times before tying the end in a knot.

A gorgeous smile lit her face. "And what is this?"

"With this ring, I pledge my heart to you. Please wait for me, Soph."

She stared at him for several moments, her eyes turning red, her throat working visibly to swallow. "I'll wait," she said hoarsely and with a wobbly smile. "I love you, William."

He dropped his forehead to hers and peered into her eyes. "I love you. Will you trust me, will you marry me?"

A sweet, shy smile curved her lips, and then she nodded happily. "I will!"

The joy in her eyes humbled him. *I will endeavor to make you the happiest of women.* And he held her in his arms and for endless hours as they laughed and chatted.

TWO WEEKS LATER...

The silence in the drawing room throbbed like a festered wound that desperately needed a lance to relieve the pain. William swallowed down the sick feeling rising inside and awaited an answer.

"I beg your pardon?" his mother finally

demanded from where she sat, elegant and ramrod-straight, on a winged back chair near the roaring fire.

Before William could reply, she shot her husband a scandalized look. "Did you also hear our son asked us permission to wed…" the words choked her as if she could not bear to utter them. "Upon my word, I cannot credit such nonsense!"

"I did," his father said in that contemplative manner of his, dark blue eyes pinned to William with the intensity of a hawk. "The heir to all my estates and grandeur wishes to marry the daughter of the local reverend."

Pronounced disappointment and menacing anger rang in his father's voice. He took up a glass which appeared to hold brandy and with calculated indifference meant to signal his dismissal of William's query, the duke made his way over to the floor-to-ceiling French windows which faced the rolling lawns of his estate.

"It was frequently remarked that you were too often in the company of Miss Knightly, but I never dared dream you would take it this far!" the duchess cried, her gaze brimming with accusation and rebuke.

His mother closed her eyes and turned her face

away from him. William's chest went tight, he made his way over to her and sat on the sofa in front of her.

He squared his shoulders. "Mother, I know you have hopes that I will marry Lord Appleby's daughter. But I do not love—"

"What do you know of love?" she snapped, jutting her chin toward him. "You are three and twenty! You've hardly lived."

"I've experienced enough of the world to be sure," he said quietly. "I am certain as the sun sets daily and the morning breaks that I love Miss Knightly. If you would meet her and—"

"I have no interest in meeting a girl who has seduced you away from your good senses because she wishes to elevate herself and her family," the duchess said with biting incivility. "People ought to know their place in this world and abide by it! A marriage between you both is quite unthinkable by our family's standard."

His father finally wrested his attention away from the lawns and faced his parents. His features were austere and foreboding. "Your mother is correct, son. We will not tolerate you blighting your future by even *thinking* to marry this girl. If you do not wish to marry Lord Appleby's daughter, that is fine," he said with a dismissive wave of his hand. "Pick another. There are many beauties in the *ton* with suitable dowries and political connections."

A yawning emptiness seemed to swell within William and threatened to swallow him. He stood, staring at the parents he loved and respected and knew he could not meet their demands. "Is your only objection because of her connections?" he asked hoarsely.

His father walked over to him and rested a hand on his shoulder. "Take her as your mistress. We'll not object to such an arrangement."

William flinched and stepped back from the embrace. "I'd never dishonor her in such a manner, Father. She is…" his throat worked on a swallow. "She is beautiful in spirit. She is gentle, kind, and a young lady of thoughtful and considerate manners."

"Be that as it may, she is only fit for one role in your life."

A mistress…

William walked away and made his way to the door. He loved Sophia beyond duty and expectations. The awareness settled through his body, warmed his soul. He'd not abandon his promises because of his family's lack of welcome.

"The reverend will not permit her to marry you. If he does, the man will feel the full force of my displeasure, and I will *ruin* his family," the duke said to William's retreating form, his tone implacable. "And if you should run away with her and bring scandal and disgrace to our family name, I shall not let you off lightly."

His father's promise cracked in the air like a whip, he faltered in his steps, and turned to face him. His mother had stood with his father, their unity in this decision evident.

"I made a promise to Miss Knightly that I would marry her," he said quietly.

"Her family would not dare sue for breach of promise," the duke said arrogantly. "I'll see to it the reverend loses his standing and income."

"I'll not dishonor my words or shame Miss Knightly," replied William.

His mother swayed, lifting a hand to her mouth, her eyes pooling with unshed tears. "So, you will shame us instead? Do you see nothing objectionable in the connection?"

"Mama, Miss Knightly's family is respectable, even if they are not wealthy. Her father is the son of a baron, and her aunt by her father married an earl.

You both professed your admiration and love for me over the years, father, yet you seem quite unconcerned now with the future state of my happiness. If I must leave with Miss Knightly, I shall, and if I must wait until she is of age to consent freely, I will."

Ignoring his mother's choked cry of protest, he made his way from the drawing room and outside to the stables, calling for his horse to be saddled. A few minutes later, he was riding toward the village and to the reverend's cottage. The first thing that struck William was how unusually quiet the streets of Mulford were today. Several shops were closed, and the normally rowdy and lively children were missing. A horse powered toward him, and he slowed his canter, smiling to see that it was his youngest brother, Simon. Soon to be Dr. Simon Astor, he corrected, a burst of pride firing inside his chest.

His brother had bravely defied his family's expectation of entering the clergy and had studied medicine to their mother's distress. He'd only recently returned for holidays from Edinburgh where he studied under a renowned surgeon and physician.

His brother slowed his horse as he drew up

beside William. He frowned at the worry that filled
Simon's dark blue eyes.

"Is all well?"

A heavy sigh issued from him. "I am exhausted
and must sleep. I have been awake for two days with
only snatches of rest."

It was then William noted the gauntness to his
face and the weariness which seemed to clung to
Simon like a second skin. He was only a lad of
twenty, quite brilliant, and sure of himself and his
place in the world. William had never seen him in
such a state of disarray. "Tell me what has
happened, and how might I help you," he offered.

A quick smile of thanks creased his brother's
face, at once lifting away the visage of an
older man.

"Dr. Powell sent a boy for me yesterday having
heard that I was recently home from my studies."

William glanced about the quiet streets, once
again, a disturbing sensation winding through his
heart. "What did he require of you?"

Simon met his gaze. "There is a sickness in the
village. Dozens of homes are affected, and there
have been a few deaths."

Shock punched William in the gut, and he

tightened his hand on the reins. "Good God, man! Say it isn't so."

"It might be cholera." This was said with grim forbearance.

William sucked in a harsh breath. "Cholera, here in Mulford?"

Since his own return from university, he had been working closely with his father and a few other lords as they drafted motions they would take to parliament. That ravaging and incurable disease had claimed over six thousand lives in London only a year past, and a reputed twenty thousand more in Paris only a few months ago. The numbers reported in Russia were astronomical, and many doctors believed it to be a wasting disease caused by foul air. There were other theories of course, but what concerned the duke was the general uncleanliness of London, and the genuine and frightening possibility that their dirty and sewage-laden streets might contribute to the terrible disease spreading even farther than the eastern slums and eventually to the west, then the whole of England.

William had been disgusted by the stench and pollution in London. In this modern age, with all the recent discoveries, it seemed so medieval. He could not understand how the great minds of the day could not see that the filth was unhealthy. He had heard the various medical theories as explanation for disease and found them wanting. The village stunk from cesspits, and open sewers; his father the Duke should have done something to make sure that everything was wholesome in Mulford. As most of the villagers were his tenants, it was the Duke's responsibility. The dukedom was wealthy enough to put in modern sewers, but his father had not been prepared to 'waste money when it was not needful to do so.'

William had discussed the matter of installing sewers in the village with Simon, and they had agreed they were necessary, but his father held the purse strings. Somehow, he had believed like many others such diseases would remain in the urban areas that were densely populated and ran amok with waste and garbage.

Cholera here in Mulford seemed so improbable, and William recalled there were several theories which claimed it was contagious from one patient to another. Dread coiled in his gut. "Are you certain it is cholera? I must inform father immediately to secure as much help as possible for the people of Mulford."

"It could also be Typhus," Simon said wearily.

"Or some other disease we are not sure of. A few of the parishioners I saw had a fever, severe nervous agitation, a weak pulse, and in the extreme case of Reverend Knightly, purging."

Ice prickled along William's skin. "The reverend is afflicted?" Good God, how was Sophia coping with her father's illness?

Simon rubbed a hand over his face and released a heavy sigh. "I fear his entire family has fallen to the disease."

For a timeless moment, William could not breathe, or think, all rational capabilities forgotten. Cold sweat slicked down his back beneath his jacket, and for precious seconds he could not utter a single word. The roaring in his eardrums became too loud, and though Simon's lips moved, William could not discern his words. Finally, the tight band across his throat loosened, and he asked, "Sophia is ill?" He hadn't seen her in a bit over a week, but when he'd left for his short trip to town she had been in robust health.

His brother sent him a sharp glance. "Miss Knightly…yes…are you intimate with the family?"

"I am."

Simon grimaced. "It is sad to say they are one of the worse afflicted families in the area. Dr. Powell and I have little hope——"

William urged his horse into a flat run as he made his way toward the rectory. He prayed, deep anguish already beating in his heart. He'd pored over dozens of reports in his father's library, preparing arguments and research along with medical reports and journals of the disease's deadly effects.

If the Knightly family and the people of Mulford were indeed suffering through a cholera outbreak, their chances of survival and recovery were quite dim. William raced toward his love and prayed as he'd never prayed before. But no hope entered his heart, only a tight ball of grief and dread that such a beautiful, vibrant soul like Sophia might die.

Please, God, save her!

CHAPTER 1

Six years and eleven months later…

"**M**arry me."

"*Yes.*"

It had been a little over an hour since his brother, Dr. Simon Astor, had walked away from Hawthorne Park's overly large dining room with William's fiancée in tow. Their mother, the duchess of Wycliffe, was still busy soothing the hysterical Countess Langford, who lamented loudly that Lady Miranda, her daughter, had brought their entire family and reputation to ruin.

William chuckled mirthlessly, refilling his glass with whisky and tipping it to his lips. The person who had brought the Cheswick family's name into question was the countess herself, who had connived to compromise William with her daughter a few weeks previously, simply because he was the 12th duke of Wycliffe.

William had gone along with the farce because he knew he needed to acquire a wife. In a few weeks, he would be thirty, and the years he had spent abroad had filled his pockets with great wealth, but his heart remained an empty husk. His duty to the title was not one he would ever neglect, but he had thought it his obligation to finally return home from India and to seek a bride to marry. The farcical affair of Lady Miranda being trapped in his chamber under his brother's roof should have rescued William from wading through the *ton* to select a suitable future duchess. It had appeared to him at the time an easy decision to acquiesce to. The fact that Lady Miranda was also an acclaimed beauty, together with being the daughter of an earl had made her seem a perfectly acceptable bride. William had believed himself very fortunate with the turn of events until his brother Simon had spoken up.

"I know your honor is very important to you, but I must explain that Lady Miranda is my Sophia."

William rubbed the aching center of his chest that had burned to life upon Simon's words. If William had known that his brother loved Lady Miranda, he would never have made the offer. He lifted his glass in a toast to the eloping couple, admiring their audacity and bravery in the face of their family's and society's expectations.

A knock sounded on the door of the library. "Enter."

The scent of his mother's lavender perfume preceded her inside. He turned from the windows and observed her progress within the lavish space. His mother was dressed in the height of fashion, even if she yet wore half-mourning. Her lavender silk dress was pin-tucked decoratively into her still tiny waist. Its full sleeves tightening into delicate black lace cuffs. The neckline and hem of the full skirts ornamented with black lace, trimmed with opulent black ribbon bows. Mourning she had defiantly worn since her husband had died more than six years earlier from a failure of his heart. William thought his mother would have continued to wear black if she had thought the color suited her, but she looked very good in grays and shades of muted purple. A color she considered most suitable for a dowager duchess. His mother made her way to the mantle and to his amusement poured herself a healthy draft of whisky. The duchess took several swallows, spluttering slightly.

"The scandal will be absolutely dreadful," she said. "Whatever was your brother thinking! The countess is still totally prostrate with grief at their selfish actions. She is so disappointed that Miranda will not be your bride and dreads facing the embarrassment that will ensue. We must do everything within our power to stem the tide of scandal!"

"The countess was abominably selfish in trying to force her daughter to marry a man she does not love. I was just as damnably foolish to go along with her plan when I merely found Miranda attractive. I was wrong to think only that it would simplify my life and avoid a tedious search to find a wife. I regret the upset caused but I cannot regret standing aside for Simon and Miranda's happiness. Simon and the lady were true to their hearts. I will do my duty and find another bride."

His mother turned an appalled gaze in his direction. "You sound as if you admire their outrageous conduct!"

William smiled briefly. "I do." Once many years

ago he, William had thought about running away with the girl he'd loved more than duty and honor. He had lost her and it still hurt him deeply. If only he hadn't dawdled, seeking to persuade his parents to allow their marriage, their lives now would be of rich and contented fulfillment together. Instead, she was bones lying somewhere in a cold, unmarked grave. "I shall use all my influence to allow them to escape any scandal."

"The countess has already sent notices to the paper of your engagement to Miranda. Now the world will know you've been jilted."

"I'll admit to being such an ogre that the fair lady could not bear to endure my company for another minute."

His mother frowned. "That will not do. Your reputation must not bear any scrutiny—"

"I am certain it will not break," he said flatly and with considerable arrogance. "I *am* the duke of Wycliffe."

"How unconcerned you are," she huffed, taking another tentative sip of her drink. "I am sure you'll be running off to town for your share of amusements, and then you'll be at the nasty end of tonight's disaster. Though I must warn you there will not be much to be done now that the Season is ending," his mother said, watching him keenly.

William made a noncommittal sound, almost alarmed at the lack of interest he felt in the excitement and amusements of the *ton*. His mind and heart were stuck remembering the burning love which had glowed in Lady Miranda's eyes for his brother, and the mistake he had almost made in intending to rob them of that happiness. "There will be enough for me to do," he said, "And I'll be assuming my duties in the House of Lords at its next opening, and so now is a good time to reacquaint myself with the lords and ladies of the *ton*."

"And you'll be doing it amidst a brewing scandal!" she cried, her voice rich with displeasure. "Lady Miranda was perfect for you! So beautiful and poised."

But far more perfect for Simon.

An irritated sigh heaved from her. "I'll have to make a list of the eligible ladies for your perusal, and perhaps plan a garden party so you can meet as many as possible. I do believe Lady Vivian, the Earl of Granville's daughter, would be absolutely perfect for you!"

William considered his mother and the smile of strain about her lips. "I thought you would prefer to make your way to Bath to see your friend as soon as possible."

Her eyes widened, and she took several sips as if to gather her composure. "You know of the viscount?"

"Simon kept me abreast of happenings at home," he said, casually admitting to his knowledge of her affair with a man ten years younger than herself.

"I believed you would have been violently opposed to the idea, William."

"I have been away for years, Mother. Who am I to oppose any desire you have in your heart?"

She glanced away briefly before leveling her gaze on him once more. "You are the duke, the head of this family. You have at last taken up the duties and responsibilities of your station in life, it was always your destiny to be the duke and take your proper place in society. Now is the time when all propriety must be observed so the family name remains unblemished."

William took a long swallow of his whisky. "Are you happy, Mother? Does he make you happy?"

"Whenever I am in Bath...my joy is indescribable," she murmured, a flush mounting on her elegantly slanted cheekbones.

His mother was quite a handsome woman at eight and forty, with no hint of greying hair or wrinkles marring her exquisite face. In her youth she had been considered to outshine all the other debutantes and her hand had been avidly sought by the handsome young men of the *ton*. His father had been several years older but she had loved him openly and ardently. William knew how greatly she had been crushed by his father's death. How long she had grieved. Sorrow clutched at William's heart as he recalled how he had not been there to support her through her mourning. He had fled England's shore only months after his father's passing because he too had lost the love of his life and had found it difficult to remain where every sight, scent, taste, and even the rain reminded him of his Sophia.

Now his mother had healed from the loss of his father, how could he object to her affair. "You've decided to stop mourning?" he asked softly.

"Unexpectedly a few months ago I realized how alone I've been, and that I've hardly visited town and Bath. I've ordered a new wardrobe. Bright colors," she said with a wobbly smile.

"Do you wish to marry the viscount?"

She inhaled a sharp breath, her hand fluttering delicately to her throat. "Marry him?"

This was asked with such alarm he could see the thought had never entered her mind. "There is no need to say more, Mother, only know that you have our blessings if you wish to marry Viscount Bunbury."

The Viscount was a man of solid character according to Simon who'd gone to the trouble of investigating him. The viscount also had a good reputation in the *ton* and had his fortune. Despite the difference in their ages, the man seemed to genuinely want to be with his mother.

She stared at him for several moments before walking over and enfolding him in a hug. William wrapped his arms around her, carefully holding the glass of whisky away.

"Though you wrote to me often, I've missed you excessively, and I am very glad you are home," she murmured. Then with another squeeze of her arms, she released him and stepped away. "You've never really explored town and its attractions. I'll stay with you until a suitable—"

"Mother, please, return to Bath," he gently insisted.

"You have been away for so long. Surely you will need my help to navigate the waters of the *ton* and—"

He took her hands between his and smiled down at her. "Mother, I shall be fine. I am experienced enough to know what I desire in my wife."

The duchess thought of this for several minutes. "Very well."

He pressed a brief kiss to her cheek and then went over to the sideboard and refilled his glass with whisky. "I will make arrangements to travel to London immediately. No one will be aware that lady Miranda and I are no longer engaged until I enter the marriage mart. I am quite certain they will not announce to anyone that they've eloped."

The duchess nodded. "I will implore you, William, to recall your oath to your father that you would not marry a lady of inferior rank, fortune, and connections."

The glass being lifted to his lips stilled as if controlled by an external force. He stared at his mother, an odd pain twisting through him and piercing the numbness which he had carried for so long.

"I am now a man of nine and twenty," he

murmured. "I made that oath to father years ago before he died." Only a few weeks after he'd lost Sophia and all the hopes he'd possessed for their future.

His mother's face took on a mutinous cast. "And you must be bound by it. To honor his memory. Your father, even in his illness, only wished to protect the family's reputation because you wanted to throw it away for that girl and—"

"Enough," he said with cutting precision. "I still recall with perfect clarity your objections to a girl I adored. I am no longer guided by sentiments or matters of the heart, so I assure you, madam, I will select the future duchess of Wycliffe while keeping in my mind my position and circumstances."

"And your promise to your father," she insisted stubbornly.

With a silent curse, he noted the strain across her lips and recalled to mind that Simon had mentioned hearing an odd beat of her heart when he had examined her for melancholia. The very idea of losing his mother to any serious illness or driving her to her sickbed with his remarks tempered him as nothing else could.

"I shall bear my duty in mind, Mama," he

murmured, lifting her hand to his lip and kissing it. "And my promise to my father."

Some of the tension eased from her shoulders.

"And promise me, William," she said fiercely, "Promise me the wife you choose will be a young lady of quality whom I can approve and will be happy to call daughter, and her family my own."

His mother was never one to lose the opportunity to sink her claws home once she sensed weakness. It would not be an awkward thing to promise, for he had no notion of seeking an alliance based on tender feelings. This would be a marriage, one of mutual convenience, respect, and honor to each other. William truly did not care if he ever grew to love his wife or not, nor did he overly examine his apathy to tender sentiments. To his way of thinking, this could be achieved with any lady from the *ton*, from a respectable family.

"I promise it," he said, frowning at the cold arrow of discomfort that traveled through him at the vow.

What if…

With an inward snarl, he rejected the very notion. He'd loved already and had lost her. To do so again he could not bear it. There would be no what if…only the simple transactions of a marriage contract to a young lady suitable to be his duchess. As he finished his conversation with his mother and made his way up the magnificent stairs to his chamber, he couldn't stop the insidious thought which curled through his heart.

What if…

MEANWHILE IN HERTFORDSHIRE…

SOPHIA LAUGHED as she rounded the corner of the lanes at breakneck speed, urging her horse to the finish line. She tugged on the reins and slowed her chestnut mare, grinning as young Tommy, Lord Portman, halted his horse, too.

"You cheated," he accused, glaring at her. "Before I reached three, you darted away like a wild thing!"

"You've impugned my honor, dare I not demand a measure of satisfaction, my lord?" she asked with a wink.

Tommy chuckled at her deliberate impudence. "There is no hope for you, my dear Sophia, and it is no wonder mother despairs of finding you a husband."

Sophia sobered and glanced in the direction of the beautiful estate perched on the hill in the distance. "We all know the reason I've not made a match has nothing to do with—"

"Your hoydenish and unenthusiastic manners?" he said, repeating a refrain made by his mother, the countess Cadenham, over the years. "You challenged me to a race and then appeared in trousers! You will have to use the servants' entrance and sneak to your chamber lest Mama sees you."

"I daresay my lack of finding a husband has more to do with my lack of connections, fortune, and family than any of my escapades," she said with a heavy sigh, lifting her face to the last rays of the lowering sun.

He flinched, and shame rushed through her. "Tommy forgive me! I never meant to imply that you are not family."

"I know," he said after a few beats. "I own we will never be able to replace what you lost, Sophia."

She was unable to speak past the knot of emotions, tightening her throat. The acute memory of all that had been lost to her always filled her with overwhelming emotions. Several years ago, a disease epidemic had ravaged the sleepy and idyllic village of Mulford and had taken her mother, sister, and father in one cruel, heartrending blow. Somehow, Sophia had survived the illness after days of battling the fever, pain, and delirium. How she had screamed and torn at her hair when the doctor had informed her of the loss of her family. Still weakened she had fainted, and upon waking she had been in a carriage with her cousins, Lydia and Tommy, and her Aunt Imogen hovering over her. They had taken her away from Mulford and the unbearably weight of all that happened there.

All the happiness had been drained from Sophia's heart, and she'd only known bleakness for an exceedingly long time. It had taken several weeks to fully recover, and as soon as she had been able, Sophia had made her way back to Mulford. The memory of trekking for miles to Hardwick Park to the man she'd loved with her soul and being turned away stabbed the pain deeper into her heart, flaming it into agony.

"I did not mean to cast you into a somber mood," the viscount said.

She pushed away the memories and buried the emotions deep under the surface of her heart.

"Please do not regard it, Tommy, I am quite fine," she said with a smile that trembled on her lips.

"Will you travel to town tomorrow? Lady Pemberley's ball is one my sister is determined not to miss. I know you are not the sort to like these events, but Lydia is keen on attending, and without you to chaperone her, Mama will find it exhausting to sustain her attendance."

Lydia was Sophia's dearest friend and Tommy's twin sister. She suspected he wanted to pursue his own amusements elsewhere and did not want the trouble of escorting his sister to the ball. For the last few Seasons, the duty to be her cousin's companion and chaperone had fallen to her shoulders, and she hadn't protested, owing much to her aunt for taking her in without fuss or questions after the tragedy. Sophia nodded and urged her horse in the direction of the stables.

"My valises and portmanteau are already packed. I'll be traveling to town with Lydia and you, Tommy," she said with gentle amusement. "I am sure Aunt Imogen will still expect you to accompany us to the ball."

"I have other plans," he said with a wink. "With a delightful widow who—"

"Tommy!" Sophia cried with a blush, knowing what the rogue had been about to say.

"Is that maidenly demureness I am detecting from a lady of five and twenty, one who fences, audaciously swims in the sea, rides astride in trousers and who I *know* kissed one Lord Sanderson last year in this very garden?"

She glared at him before laughing. Sophia had fallen lamentably short of expectation time and time again as she lived her life as if there were no promise of tomorrow.

"*When I grow old, I would like to swim in the sea,*" her thirteen-year-old sister Henrietta had said wistfully as she had stared at the crashing waves at the seaside town in Brighton one summer.

"*I daresay I would like to ride astride one day, in trousers!*" their mama had said with a chortle as they had named the adventures they would partake in if not for society's expectations and eventual censure, "*and even sell my paintings.*"

That had been said with an expression of desperate hunger. Her mother had a talent which few could aspire to, but Papa had thought it unladylike and vulgar to actually sell her work. What would people say? That phrase had been a common rebuke from his lips.

Sophia's father had looked on indulgently, with a smile on his face, and had shocked them all by saying, "*I would partake in a horse race with the best of them all. Mayhap a carriage race with the rakes and rogues of London!*"

"*And I would like to marry Lord Lyons*," Sophia had boldly said to the utter shock of her parents, and the delight of her sister.

Sophia had distressed her aunt as she had endeavored to live her life freely, fulfill all the desires her family had held in their hearts, doing their adventures for them. As she accomplished each one, she would lie on the grass and stare at the heavens and whisper, "*Mama, Papa, Henrietta…. I did this…*" and spend a couple hours speaking to her departed family.

While she lived her life on the edge of society's censure, loneliness had crammed her heart full. The few times her aunt had tried to broach the topic of her finding a husband to marry she had shied away from the conversation. She had rejected the notion of ever forming such a lasting attachment. Marriage and a family were no longer in the cards for her. She had lost her family years ago, and Sophia could not bear the idea of letting anyone get that close again, to avoid repetition of such brutal loss and pain.

But she wanted to enjoy life to its fullest and all its offerings. Lately, she had been wondering about the pleasures of the flesh, she admitted with a guilty flush mounting her cheeks. And it had a lot to do with the passionate embrace in which she had caught Tommy with one of his lady loves at a country rout last year. A surge of longing had filled her heart and tears had pricked behind her lids as she'd watched them. Then she had turned away, wishing to give them some privacy.

Memories of being in William's arms had haunted her throughout that night, and when Lord Sanderson had whisked her onto the terrace and away from curious eyes, she had allowed him a kiss. Nothing had been roused in her breast, and with shock she had pulled away from the man. When William had kissed her, she had flamed in his embrace. Could it be that grief and pain had killed all desires in her heart and body?

Sophia urged her horse into a canter, truly wondering if she could continue the wildly improper avenues her musing had been merrily taking her. *An affair*. One of utter discretion before she put her most exciting plan into effect. She would depart from England's shores for Europe for another grand adventure. Or perhaps she should wait until she reached Versailles and then find herself a lover.

Utter madness, she chided herself, nudging her horse into a run toward the stables. The only thing she needed to concentrate on at the moment was ensuing her dear Lydia had a wonderful time in London, and to help her secure a proper match by the end of the Season.

Nothing more.

Once in the forecourt, she dismounted and handed over the horse to a stable lad, and quickly snuck inside. The butler, Mr. Ormsby, showed no reaction to her manner of dress. Sophia hurried down the long hallway, and then up the winding stairs when her aunt's voice halted her from below.

"Sophia?"

She closed her eyes briefly before turning around and peering down. "Yes, Aunt Imogen?"

Aunt Imogen held a vase of flowers—dahlias—in her hand. Her aunt's gaze skipped over the trousers, half-boots, and white shirt she wore. Disapproval furrowed her brows for a few seconds before she sighed.

"And whose outrageous dream are you acting out today?"

A lump formed in Sophia's throat and she wanted to rush down the stairs and fling herself into her aunt's embrace. Years ago, when a few of their neighbors had called her manners wild and improper, Sophia had explained tearily to her aunt that she wanted to live every dream her family had ever had but had been too afraid to explore. Her aunt had struggled to understand, but she too had missed her brother dreadfully, and had allowed Sophia her eccentricities. She had done her best to be discreet when warranted and had even offered to rent her own cottage with the inheritance of five hundred pounds from her father so as not to be a burden to her aunt's household with her more flamboyant ways. Her aunt had refused but had never shown such understanding before.

"It was Mama's own," she said, after taking a steady breath. "She...she had mentioned it once before when we were by the seaside, but in her diary.... she often spoke of being free to race across the moors, feeling the wind of her face as the horse thundered beneath her."

There was a contemplative air about her aunt as she considered Sophia.

"Well then, I am quite glad you experienced that, I do urge you to keep in mind that we have guests." Then she smiled and continued toward the drawing room.

With a smile, Sophia hurried to her room and stripped off the trousers and shirt. She stood in her knee-length drawers, corset and chemisette. She rang the bell for help with her corset and bounded breasts, but it was Lydia who arrived.

"Mama mentioned what she caught you in," Lydia said with a wide smile, ambling over to tug at the tight laces.

Sophia released a sigh of relief as the whale boned corset loosened and the bindings were removed. It had been tempting not to wear restrictive garments, but her breasts were too bountiful for her to be racing across the country without it. That would have been shocking and scandalous, and possibly even Tommy would have rebuked her behavior.

Lydia sat on the chaise longue by the window, a bright gleam in her expressive brown eyes. "I am terribly excited to be going to London tomorrow. This is my second Season, and I do hope it promises to be more fruitful than my first one! I've been missing for so long; I daresay all the *beaux* who'd been so promising are no longer on the marriage mart."

Lydia was three and twenty but was only entering her second Season due to a long bout of an infection of the lungs. Aunt Imogen had taken her to the country for fresh air and recovery a little over two years ago, and Lydia was quite keen on returning to town to reacquaint herself with the elegancies and frivolities of town life. Sophia had been her companion and friend for the last few years, and while she did not enjoy the offerings of the *ton*, she was quite happy to be there to support her friend.

"I'll try not to hover much as your chaperone," she said teasingly. "Perhaps you'll finally be able to get that kiss you have been dreaming of."

Lydia predictably blushed and tucked a strand of her vibrant red hair behind her ears. "Only if Lord Jeremy Prendergast is still unmarried! I did like him so very much when we met. But if not, I'll certainly not make a cake of myself and wear my heart on my sleeve. Another suitable lord will do for I am quite determined to secure a wonderful match by next month!"

Sophia tugged a light blue day dress from the

armoire and peeked around the dress at Lydia. "Within a month?"

"Yes," Lydia cried in mock horror. "I am three and twenty, a veritable spinster." Then she toed off her slippers and folded her feet onto the chaise. "Do you not wish to be married, Sophia? I cannot believe you do not hunger for a man of your own….and children…and best of all to be the mistress of your own home!"

I do not dream anymore.

But she dared not say it, hating to do anything to take that shine from Lydia's eyes.

"If someone suitable were to present himself, I might consider it," she said with a light laugh. *For an affair…nothing more.*

That excited Lydia, who jumped to her feet, grabbed Sophia's hand and tugged her to the bed. Sophia spent the next hour, laughing and making a list with Lydia on the kind of gentlemen who might be suitable.

No rakes. Not even the reformed ones.

He must be no older than two and thirty.

Must have a noteworthy title.

Sophia had rolled her eyes at that one, and Lydia had remarked nothing less than a viscount would do for her mother.

His kisses must be pleasant.

And at that…Sophia had shocked and titillated Lydia by saying, "If a kiss from your *beau* does not make your heart tremble and fire flames from your belly…. he will not do."

When Lydia had demanded more, Sophia had declined, but for the first time for some many years, that night she had dreamed again of William's kisses.

CHAPTER 2

London, one week later…

Wiliam frowned into his drink, searching the amber liquid as if it would answer the question as to why he was in Lady Harman's garden and not inside twirling a young lady across the parquet ballroom floor. He'd been at the ball for over an hour, and no sense of excitement or anticipation thrilled through him at the notion of chatting with the pretty young ladies to help him determine who best to call upon tomorrow.

He was uninspired about starting the courtship dance. With a grimace, he knocked back the whisky in his glass, appreciating the smooth burn as it slid down his throat and warmed his belly. This apathy toward seeking a wife had to end. William knew that it was his duty to ensure the succession that he could not avoid. He feared if he left it for much longer, it would be impossible to drum up any sort of interest to get the deed done.

The din of laughter and music spilled into the night, signaling that one of the wide terrace doors had been opened.

A large hand slapped William on the shoulder, and he turned around with a start of surprise.

Unfathomable dark gray eyes peered at him, and a familiar crooked smile.

"Worsley?"

"Good God, you really are here! I heard a few whispers about town and in the card rooms just now, but I did not believe it." Viscount Worsley embraced him in a surprising hug.

"It seemed I was more missed that I imagined," William said drily, but returned the man's embrace, a sense of belonging shifting through him.

They released each other, and the somber jadedness in Worsley's eyes had William arching a brow.

They made their way inside, and he ignored the

sensations of the walls closing in on him at the crush of ladies and gentlemen milling in every direction, filling all the public rooms of Lady Harman's home.

"How have you been, Worsley?" William asked, accepting a glass of champagne from a passing footman. Another glass of whisky would have been better, but for now, the bubbly drink would suffice until he retired to the card room.

Worsley had been one of his good friends at University, though they had been like night and day in their characters. The viscount even then had possessed an air of profligacy for a young gentleman and had made no effort to suppress his rakish ways despite his father's anger.

"The same," he said, taking a sip of his drink. "Heard that you have been in India these past few years."

"Only for three. Spent some time in Calcutta and Bombay. Then I went on to Egypt. Then spent some time in France and Rome researching and investing in new business interests."

They stared at each other for a bit, and it was as if Worsley understood William's silent words, that he'd been restless and seeking for a happiness that never came. That he had busied himself with business opportunities when he had enough wealth to last him several lifetimes. It wasn't that he hadn't lived. He'd done so with the best of them in each exotic place he visited and stayed for several months, but there was always that hole that no amount of drinking, women, or work had been able to fill.

"And are you in England to stay?"

"I am."

"Ah," Worsley said, knowledge gleaming in his eyes. "Planning on finding a wife then and settling down?"

William parted his lips to speak and faltered as if someone had ripped the words away from him. A slow jerk of his heart, then his mouth went dry. A young lady stood on the sidelines of the ballroom, speaking to another young miss. The lady who had captured his attention had her back turned to him, but there was something about her stance, which seemed so familiar. More than familiar, for without seeing her face, his interest had stirred.

"Do you know her?" the viscount asked, his tone shaded with amusement and a bit of envy. As if he saw a conquest he wanted for himself, and

William's unexpected reaction was waylaying his dissolute plans.

"No," William said with a frown, unable to explain the drumming of his heart or the sudden shakiness of his hand. "The slope of her back…the way in which she canted her head…there! She did it again. It reminds me of someone. Someone I once knew."

"The way you are staring at whoever that young lady may be, is enough to incite considerable speculation and gossip."

Despite the viscount's warning, William walked away, and descended the curving staircase, keeping the lady in his line of sight always. She wore a peach-colored evening gown trimmed with gold lace and ribbons, with matching peach gloves and delicate dancing slippers. Her dress bared the creamy swell of her shoulders which accentuated her exquisite shape.

She shifted slightly, glancing at the dancers on the floor. Her lips curved in a slight smile, one that appeared…sad and hauntingly lovely to William, and so familiar.

"*Ah Christ*," he murmured, his heart now a war drum thudding noisily inside his chest. It was the way that she tucked a wisp of her brown hair with golden highlights behind her ears. The sleek way she angled her head to indicate she was listening to her friend's animated chatter. Then it was the wide smile which curved her lips. Familiar and enchanting. William stood frozen, closing his hand so tightly over the glass of champagne that it shattered.

"Good God, man, what is it?" Lord Worsley said, coming over to stand beside William while beckoning to a footman to attend to the mess.

Blood dripped from the side of his hand, and William did not care. The only thing that mattered was moving closer to the lady who reminded him of *her*. It couldn't be her....it could not be, yet every emotion that had been locked underneath the deliberately hardened surface of his heart broke through on an anguished roar.

It was her. He could feel it...but it was impossible. For a terrible, timeless minute, he could do nothing but stare as a decidedly odd weakness assailed him.

"Sophia," he finally said her name aloud, needed his voice to order him against the foolish hope beating inside his heart.

The lady stiffened, and it was then he realized his closeness. Bracing himself to offer an apology for his impertinence or to fall on his knees in gratitude, he said, "Sophia…Miss Knightly."

A STARTLING SENSE of recognition prickled over Sophia.

That voice.

It belonged to the man she had loved with every fragment of her broken heart. It belonged to the man she heard in her dreams, and it belonged to the man whom she had long given up on ever meeting again in this lifetime. The raw emotions tearing through her were wholly unexpected…for she must be mistaken. She felt afraid to turn around, and dear Lydia stared behind her with an expression of awe and delight, which only meant the gentleman was 'handsome as sin.'

A warm gloveless hand clasped her upper arm. The wildly improper touch jolted her, and a tremble went through her entire body.

"Sophia...is it really you?"

The question was in a low, rough, and overly intimate murmur.

Ladies had begun to gawp and whisper behind

their fans. She felt too vulnerable to look behind her. Lydia and Aunt Imogen stared, their eyes wide with shock and their lips formed perfect 'O's of surprise.

Her cousin's gaze flickered to the hand which still clasped Sophia's arm so scandalously. She couldn't pull away, though she wanted to and to berate whoever it was for their lack of good manners in such a public setting.

"Will you not face me?"

It was a command, and she slowly turned. The world fell from beneath her feet, her throat burned, and her eyes filled with tears. The ache in her chest became a physical thing, and there was no ease in its tightening grip. He was so very handsome, with the firm set of his chin, piercing dark blue eyes, and sensually firm lips. It was hard to see the boy she had loved in the man who now gazed down at her. He seemed hardened, his eyes so much older as if he'd been ravaged by a pain that he'd hardly been able to bear.

The tension in him was palpable, and his eyes darkened with dangerous heat. His black evening trousers fitted splendidly to his lean waist, powerful thighs, and long muscular legs. His jacket and waistcoat molded quite closely to his broad shoulders. The sudden tremble in her heart was appalling. "Wil…William?"

He stared at her with ill-concealed shock, his hand fell away as if he had been singed by the hottest fire. They stared at each other for several moments, a perilous tension heavy on the air.

"I perceive that you are acquainted with his Grace," her aunt said softly, after hurrying to her side in a welcoming show of support. "However, I will affect an introduction as the entire room is all aflutter with this display!"

"Your Grace," her aunt began, "Allow me to introduce my niece, Miss Sophia Knightly. Sophia—"

"I…I am terribly sorry, Aunt Imogen, I must leave," Sophia gasped.

She hurriedly dipped into a curtsey and whirled around. Sophia ignored Lydia's curious and horrified stare.

Sophia pushed through the throng who craned their heads to follow her as she moved as fast as she could toward the door leading to the hallway. Several whispers floated behind her, but she could not bear to pause long enough to listen. She jostled a footman and the tray of champagne tumbled to the floor with a resounding crash. She muttered an apology but did not stop. The whispers became more rabid and Sophia moved even faster.

Once in the hallway, she gathered the sides of her dress and broke into a run. The butler opened the door at her approach, a look of shock blooming on his face. Not daring to wonder at his expression she hurtled through it and down the steps with reckless haste. Then she ran past the line of parked carriages on Grosvenor Street, and a few shocked faces.

Memories crowded her mind and chased her as she ran away. The memory of his taste, the feel of his lips on hers, the fleeting caress of his fingers on her breast, that halting touch on the softness of her inner thighs. The deep love which had been in her heart washed over her, along with the total loss of hope and abject grief.

"Oh, God, please! Let it stop," she cried into the night as she ran harder.

Panting she slowed, pressing a hand over her mouth. A hand grabbed her from behind, and she whirled around, glancing about, gladdened to see that the street was empty. It was only her and the duke, and a darkened street barely lit by gas lamps. "You followed me," she accused, hating how her heart leaped with something fierce and wholly unexpected. It felt suspiciously like joy.

"You ran as if the devil chased you," he said, raking his fingers through his midnight strands.

"Did he not?"

"I had to chase you."

"No, you did not," she said, hating that tears gathered in her eyes like a storm that could not be suppressed.

He stepped closer, and he took her into his arms by slipping an arm around her waist and pulling her into his body.

"William!"

He pressed his mouth to hers....and it was so unexpectedly gentle that her tensed body relaxed as if it had a will beyond her own. His soft and very chaste embrace was a mere meeting of breath, yet his kiss tasted like heaven, his touch felt like regret. She guarded herself against the pleasure tingling through her. "Do you think we'll not see each other for so many years and then start back where we left off?" she asked in a choked whisper against his mouth.

He lifted his lips from hers and gathered her into a fierce hug. She pressed her face into his chest, inhaling his masculine scent deep into her lungs, and returned his scandalous embrace.

"Did you stop loving me?" he asked gruffly.

She wrenched from his arms. "How can you ask me this? We have not seen each other in almost seven years! I am no longer a girl of eighteen with foolish and impossible dreams in her heart. I've changed…. you have changed…and our lives are different. How dare you ask me that?"

"Sophia…please, answer me. Have you stopped loving me?" he asked gently as if she did love him still that would solve everything when all seemed a jumbled mess. As if the years and all the experiences they had undergone apart would be nothing in the face of a love which had proved constant.

"Yes!" she whispered fiercely. "You left me…. I lost everyone and everything, and when I called for you, William, you were not there. For my sanity…I *had* to stop loving you."

His throat worked on a swallow, and his eyes glittered with something thoroughly primal and a bit intimidating.

"Please, leave me be," she whispered, her breath hitching on a sob. A spasm of anguish snaked through her. "You are my past…please stay there."

He dropped his hand, every emotion in his gaze shuttering, and she felt the cold pierce deep into her bones. Sophia could not bear to look into his eyes. She turned and fled into the night, grateful her aunt's townhouse was only a few doors away, desperate to be away from the duke, and the riotous emotions tumbling through her with such terrible force, and the scandal they had just caused.

CHAPTER 3

Sophia pressed a hand to her chest, hoping to calm her thoughts and ease the furious pounding in her heart. Hours later and the years had still fallen away as if they had never parted. She felt trapped in the past, the memories of William's kisses, illicit touches, and fervent promises of a forever kind of love haunting her. So many questions had kept her tossing wide awake. *Where had William been? Why had he left...where did he go, and what was he thinking with his outrageous questions?* And how dare he kiss her as if seven years and so many unknowns had not separated them.

I am silly! She fiercely scolded herself. There was no reason to allow herself to be so out of sorts.

Another knock sounded on the door, and she

closed her eyes, hating her cowardice. After taking several steady breaths, she said hoarsely. "Please, come in."

The door opened, Lydia walked in, then gently closed the door. "So, you know his Grace?" she asked, cutting painfully into the heart of the matter.

There was no mention that Sophia had been hiding in her chamber for the better part of the day, refusing to go downstairs for breakfast or luncheon. "I do."

Lydia pushed from the door, an expression of hurt crossing her face. "When? How? You've never mentioned him before and the rumors that exploded after he ran after you last night were that he had been away from England for about six years. You came to live with us right after the—" her lips closed on 'tragedy.'

"It was before…I knew him before and Lydia…" Sophia clasped her overheated cheeks between her hands. "I love you, and I promise one day I shall tell you everything that happened between myself and William, but not today."

Lydia's eyes widened. "William?"

Sophia's entire body blushed. Before she could respond, Lydia hurried over to the small valise on the bed.

"What is the meaning of this?"

"I…" she raked her fingers through her tousled hair. "I must return to Hertfordshire for a few days. I…he is *here*…in town. His presence was so very unexpected. When we first came to London years ago for your first Season, I dreaded seeing him. Then I came to realize he had truly left and might never return. Or he might be here, but I was simply inconsequential to him, and I had too much pride and my heart was too shattered for me to ever return to his home and seek him again."

Lydia's face softened. "We can stay in for a few days, you do not have to leave."

"And if he should call on me here? He is a duke! Aunt Lydia would not dare snub him."

Scandalized dismay crossed Lydia's face. "He would not dare call upon you after the scandal he caused. And Mama also mentioned that last week, *the Morning Chronicles* announced that he was engaged to Lady Miranda Cheswick."

"He is to be married!"

"He certainly did not act the part last night, and society is all aflutter. Are you certain you do not wish to stay? Your departure might fan the flames of the scandal."

"Or my absence might douse the flames

considering I am quite inconsequential to society." Sophia's throat went tight, and she tried very hard not to think about the newspaper announcement that William was engaged. *It is none of my concern!* "I promise to return soon, Lydia. I know how much being in town means to you. I...I need to speak with your Mama for a bit. I...I...need to return to the country, just for a few days."

Lydia nodded, and Sophia exhaled with relief, her heart gladdened that Lydia did not berate her for wanting to visit the graves of her family.

"I'll speak with Aunt Imogen and ask for a carriage and a maid to accompany me. Please bear with Tommy and Aunt as your chaperones until I return."

Lydia smiled and made to leave, paused at the door and without turning said, "I've never known you to run away from anything before, Soph. It's not like you at all."

She flinched but had no rebuttal. She *was* running, and she was deathly afraid to examine her heart for the reasons. Sophia was following one instinctual feeling now, and it was that wild voice inside crying,

Run as far as you can!

WILLIAM SAT in the cold silence of his library before a roaring fire that did not warm him. His mind was warring with the desire inside, urging him to chase after Sophia. He'd visited the countess's townhouse only yesterday, for he had been unable to banish the urgent need to speak with her, only to discover that Sophia had chosen to flee to the countryside of Hertfordshire.

Let me go...you are my past.

That impassioned plea had torn his chest open. And now he had to accept that she had run far away from him. William's thoughts had been thrown into total disorder. How could it be that she was alive? He had confessed to her aunt that he once loved her and would like to rekindle a friendship. He had apologized for his conduct at the ball. It seemed all the news sheets in town had run with the story and had wildly speculated as to the manner of relationship between the Duke of Wycliffe, and Miss Sophia Knightly. They had also seen fit to mention that it had been recently announced he was engaged to marry Lady Miranda Cheswick. There had been numerous discussions over what that lady thought of the latest development involving her fiancé.

He had penned a reply to the *Gazette*, declaring that Lady Miranda had recently married Dr. Simon Astor, his brother, and it was a love match which William fully supported. The scandal sheets seemed disinclined to speculate on that; instead, they kept on with their insinuations on the type of relationship he might have had with Sophia…and who exactly was Miss Knightly, they wanted to know.

Her Aunt had been polite if a bit cautious. It had not taken him long before he had charmed her over tea. He coaxed her to reveal where Sophia had fled to and she had confessed Sophia had run to her country home in Hertfordshire where she had lived for the past several years.

It should be enough to him that she was alive. For the four days following his discovery that she was alive, William had been trying to convince himself that it *was* enough. As he'd watched Sophia that night running away like a waif in the fog-shrouded night, a profound thankfulness had swept through him, and he'd been shocked to discover his eyes were damp.

Sophia was alive, and it should be sufficient…

except it simply wasn't. The hand that lifted the glass of whisky to his lips trembled fiercely and William closed his eyes briefly.

"You're alive," he murmured, hoping that saying it aloud would banish some of the strangeness that had gripped him in its relentless hold. He had hardly slept since he had seen her, and he felt as if he would never be able to close his eyes again.

All those years he had wasted grieving; all those years wasted apart. All those other women he had taken to his bed, hoping to bury the memory of her smile and sweetness. A snarl of anger slipped from him, and he hated that he felt as he if he'd betrayed the vows, he had made her. It had taken William three years after Sophia's 'death' before he had taken a lover. And it still hadn't been easy. And over that long time, he had enjoyed at least seven or eight lovers. He could hardly recall their names and faces but he had not been despoiling innocents. His lovers had come to him willingly for they all had been widows and they had found common comfort in each other.

He had been riddled with guilt and pain for years, and all this time, she had been alive. His mother had lied to him. It was the duchess who had broken the news to him that the reverend and his entire family had been lost to the disease. William realized she had done more than simply lied…for when he had raced to Mulford and had seen the list of names of all those who had died tacked to the ancient door of Reverend Knightly's former church Miss Sophia Knightly had been listed along with the reverend, his wife, and her sister. William had fallen to his knees, and he had roared out his anguish for Sophia and all the lives that had been so unfairly taken.

It had been Simon who had helped him to his feet and tried to talk some rational sense into him while he'd wept shamelessly into his brother's arms. William had rushed to the rectory, which had been as silent as a tomb. There had been no sign of life, and he had spent two days there lying in her bed which had been stripped of its sheets and all signs that she had ever rested her head there.

A wave of icy anger curled its way around his heart. His mother, a woman he still loved and had then respected, had manipulated his fears and distractions. When the epidemic had struck, he had insisted on helping Dr. Powell and Simon to treat the patients, and he had lingered by Sophia's side for several days, mopping her brow and reading poetry to her while she had tossed in fever not recognizing him. The memory of her agitation and groans of pain still had the power to ravage him. Then his father had collapsed, and his fear for his father had dragged him from Sophia's side for several days.

And somehow, his mother had conspired to use her influence during those dreadful days to deceive him.

A knock sounded on the door, and he bid enter. His butler entered.

"Your brother and his wife have called, your Grace. I've shown them to the yellow drawing room and Mrs. McGinnis is arranging for refreshments to be served."

Pleasure warmed his chest. He had not seen Simon since he had left Hawthorne Park with Lady Miranda a few weeks past. Nor had he heard from him.

"Thank you, I'll go to him." He launched himself to his feet and replaced his now empty glass on the desk. William left his library and made his way down the hall before turning left to the drawing room. The beautiful Lady Miranda stood in front of Simon and peered up at him with a loving smile as she tenderly brushed a lock of hair from his forehead. Their lips moved, but William was unable to discern their words.

"Simon," he greeted, walking over to them.

The couple turned to face him, and it was if he could see the strings of love which bound them together. No regret shone in their eyes that they had disappointed their families' expectations by eloping.

"Lady Miranda," William said with a small smile. "Have you dined? Dinner will be announced in a little over an hour's time, and I would be pleased if you would both join me."

"Ah," Simon said, blue eyes, very much like William's, twinkling. "You are not disappointed in us?"

His tone indicated that he would not care one jot if William answered yes.

"No, I am proud," he said gruffly, enfolding his brother in a hug. Over Simon's shoulder, William winked at Lady Miranda. She had the gall to roll her eyes.

How rude, he mouthed, and she laughed. And he was glad for it, and hoped they would soon mend whatever tension and misunderstanding still existed between them. He had been an ass to go along with her mother's plan to compromise them both by locking them in together.

He pulled away from his brother. "Is all well?"

Simon shared a speaking glance with his wife, and William arched a brow.

"We saw the news sheets. Good God, man, Miss Knightly is alive?"

"Let's get comfortable, and then we'll talk."

A few minutes later they were seated on comfortable sofas, more logs had been cast onto the fire, and Mrs. McGinnis had served Simon and Miranda with ratafia, and a decanter of brandy had been left for William. They had an hour before dinner would be served, and he quickly told them what had happened.

"Mother lied?" Simon demanded faintly, gripping his glass of wine. "By God, I cannot credit she would behave in such a dishonorable manner."

"Yes. I suspect she bribed the sexton. The reverend himself had died, who else would know it was a lie? And she is a duchess. Her influence is far-reaching. I know she objected to my attachment to Miss Knightly, but I never imagined she would go that far. If you recall father had fallen ill, and I was dragged to his bedside for several days. Each time I thought to leave Hawthorne Park, Mother would descend into hysterics, crying Father might die when I was gone. I ended up being away from

Sophia for a while, and I believed all to be well since you were by her side along with Dr. Powell and Dr. Campbell, and I had received no bad report."

Simon scrubbed a hand over his face. "I was there when the reverend and his wife went to their rewards. They died within a few minutes of each other, but the two girls lingered on. I spent a few days at Hawthorne Park resting, for I had worked myself to the bones, and I had to pack for my return to Edinburgh to complete my studies. When I visited the rectory, it was empty, the place devoid of any signs of life that people I knew had lived there. I found Dr. Powell in the parish hall treating several parishioners, and he informed me the girls had also passed. I never…" Simon cleared his throat. "I never imagined a man of my profession could be so wretched and complicit."

William took a healthy swallow of his drink. "Mother was cruel and vile, and she held steadfast with her deception in the face of my grief. I cannot reconcile her actions with the woman I know."

Simon grew pensive. "Will you be able to forgive her?"

"I do not know."

Lady Miranda, who had listened with an

expression of aching sympathy said, "But what happened to Miss Knightly?"

William stood and sauntered over to the windows overlooking the small side garden. "I do not know. When I saw her...she ran from me."

"And you gave chase," Simon murmured. "Your scandal has quite overshadowed the fact my wife is no longer engaged to you, and we've practically escaped society's censure unscathed."

William nodded at that assessment. "And I am glad for it."

A comfortable silence lingered.

"What will you do?" Lady Miranda queried. "I...if I might be so bold as to question if you still love her?"

Everything inside William went quiet, and he found he did not know the answer. He loved the sweet, gentle girl he remembered. The woman before him that night had been different. Her beauty had a boldness...a defiance that not been present when he knew her. How her eyes had flashed with such depths of emotion...

"I loved the girl I knew," he admitted hoarsely.

"Will you marry her?" Simon asked.

"Marry her?" Lady Miranda gasped.

Simon cast a glance at his wife. "Would that be so unusual, my love?"

She stood and made her way over. "*Years* have passed. Her feelings may no longer be attached to William. Miss Knightly might even be attached to someone else, and even William said he loved the girl he knew *then*. Perhaps on closer acquaintance now, your brother might even realize Miss Knightly is in his past."

Regrets gnawed at him without mercy. If he hadn't left England, surely he would have discovered his mother's duplicity years ago. He was at a place in his life where he wanted a wife, and now that he had rediscovered Sophia, it was unthinkable to even consider another woman. It had always been her. Yet she had been right. Years separated them…and they were very now different people. They could not go on as they had before, but he could not let her go either. The very idea was unpardonable.

Now what? A deep still voice asked him. And everything inside of him that had been empty and cold answered, *I want to know the woman she is now.*

CHAPTER 4

Hertfordshire, A few days later…

A fairy by the river side. If such magical creatures truly existed, Sophia Knightly at this moment personified one. She stood by the snaking river abutting her aunt's country estate, the sunlight cutting through the thick canopy of trees to beam direct light on her. The white of her simple day dress and golden ribbon around her waist glistened iridescently. Her hair tumbled over her shoulders and down her back in loose waves, its dark brown lustrous beauty with hints of dark and light blonde strands moving gently in the breeze. Her feet were bare of walking shoes and stockings, and at a glance William saw they were casually splayed out on the grass. She held something in her hands, and he strolled forward carefully, not wanting to disturb her tranquillity, but wanting to be closer. He needed to be closer to her.

At the oddest moments, shock would dart through him as he realized fully she was still truly alive. Perhaps if he went closer, Sophia would disappear like ashes in the wind, and he would never see her again. That had been his darkest thought as he'd traveled down from town after receiving the countess's instructions on how to find her niece. Pushing away his foolish fears, he moved close enough until he could see what she held between her thumbs.

It was the ring he'd given her so many years ago. A farce really, for it had been but a loose string from his jacket. She'd kept it...all these years. The jumble of emotions hammering at his heart—pain, gladness, bewilderment—had him closing his eyes for a few seconds. He snapped them open, not wanting to miss another moment of her.

She shifted slightly and tilted her face to the slanting rays of the sun. Her pain and uncertainty were etched on her face as if rendered by a loving artist's delicate brush. His damn heart ached. William wanted to go to Sophia and crush her into his arms, but he was afraid of frightening her. He was afraid he might kiss her senseless, afraid he might roar with anger at the years they'd miss, and afraid he would never let her go.

She closed her palm over the string ring for a few moments, bowed her head, then opened her palm and tossed it into the waters of the river. Unexpected loss tore through him with such force it almost drove him to his knees. She was saying goodbye, closing whatever feelings she'd left unresolved in her heart and resolving to forget what they'd shared.

***

Splash!

Sophia gasped, her hand fluttering to her throat as she watched William, with a few powerful strokes, make his way to the piece of string that was rapidly floating away on the currents of the water.

"William," she cried, running along the grassy embankment. "What are you doing?"

He swiped at something in the water, then placed it in his top pocket, before twisting around and swimming back toward her, fighting the rough currents of the river. Her knees wobbled, and it was difficult to admit she was quite relieved he had recovered that piece of string. Tears pricked behind her lids and the memories crowded her senses. Memories of his soft and then sometimes forceful, desperate kisses upon her lips as he'd spoken promises she'd never thought he would keep. The conviction in his voice and eyes as he'd twined it around her finger. The hours he'd held her while they'd watched the glory of the lowering sun sinking out of view and then the stars appearing in the sky above. The respect and care he'd had for her body, even though she had been willing to gift him her virtue.

Where have you been, William? Why did you leave without saying farewell?

"You are so foolish!" she cried with passionate alarm. "Rain fell throughout the night, and the rivers are swollen! Why would you risk your life for a piece of string?"

Chest heaving from the vigorous swim, he hauled himself from the waters. He made his way over to her and stopped perilously close. The hem of her dress lightly caressed his soaked boots, but she did not step away, and could only stare at him helplessly.

Instead of answering, he demanded roughly,

"Why did you throw it away?"

"It is a piece of string," she began dismissively. "I—"

"You kept it for more than six years. *Six* years, Soph."

The silence which fell between them was fraught with intimate peril. She fought to maintain an air of casual indifference. Their time together was over, and she would not allow him to rip back open wounds which had finally healed. "It does not signify that I kept it, only that I was willing and able to discard it."

A dark, haunting flash in his eyes showed before his gaze hooded. A part of her wanted to throw herself at him, demand that he hold her and explain where he'd been during those desolate years. But if she did ask him, it would mean that she still cared, that the echoes of their love and need they'd had for each other still survived unaltered within her.

He cupped her cheeks with both of his hands and lifted her face to his. The water still clinging to his hands was insufficient to cool the desperate need which suddenly burned through her. She fought not to close her eyes and reveal just how much she yearned for his touch.

"I thought you were dead."

Sophia jerked, shock arrowing through her heart. "I beg your pardon?"

"I thought you were dead," he repeated, shadows of anguish darkening his eyes, his fingers tightening imperceptibly on her cheeks. "All these years, I believed the girl I loved was lost to me. It was only when I saw you at Lady Huntley's ball, that I knew you still lived."

"Dear God!" she said, searching his eyes where she only discerned truth. An awareness filled her that he had grieved for her with his entire heart, just as she had mourned her family. Sophia stepped back from him, and he lowered his arms.

"William…please explain."

"I was by your side for a few days as you fought the disease. But I had to leave your side for my father had fallen ill."

Her lips parted, and her knees weakened. "You sang to me…and prayed for me. I…I thought it was a vision brought on by my delirium."

So many of the beliefs and suppositions she'd long held cracked and shattered at her feet. "Why did you believe me to be dead?" Sophia was unable to credit why he should have thought it to be so.

"While with my father, my mother informed me of your passing."

Another blow that had her leaning against a large beech tree for support.

Their eyes locked together and, in his gaze, she saw the raw anger and regret he was feeling.

"I hurried down to the village of Mulford, and the sexton confirmed he had buried you along with your family. He said he had not waited for your uncle or any of your family members as it had become practice for those taken by cholera to be interred immediately."

He did not need to say much more, for she fully understood the duplicity and cruelty of the duchess who had never approved of their attachment. Their love, which had burned so deeply, had not fitted into the duchess's plans, so she had determined to tear them apart.

In the depths of her despair, she had reached for him, had walked for hours to reach his stately home atop the hill, only to be given a scathing set down by the duchess which still remained vividly with her today.

"You are a lightskirt my son has been dallying with for some time now. How dare you presume to call at my home for him?"

She'd stood frozen, and confused, her mind hazed with grief, desperately wanting him to hold her. The memory continued unasked for.

"William—"

"Impudent miss! He is Lord Lyons to you!"

"Please, may I see him?" She had requested with a desperate hope.

The duchess's expression had been cold and foreboding as she'd stared down her elegant nose at Sophia.

"He is no longer living at Hawthorne Park. In fact," she had spat with deep satisfaction. *"He is no longer in England."*

Sophia had stumbled back as if she'd been pushed. *"He…he left?"* Without saying goodbye or coming to see me? Had been her silent cry, one the duchess had seen.

"My son bid his farewell to those who were important to him." Then she had spun around and called for the butler. *"See her out,"* the duchess had snapped with an air of cold authority. *"She is not to be allowed on the grounds of Hawthorne Park ever again."*

The shame and confusion she had felt then washed over her senses. She hadn't seen William that day, or any other in the years since. The remembered feeling of helplessness and powerlessness scythed through her. She had been crushed…devastated, and it had taken so much strength and determination for her to forge herself into the woman that she was today.

"I am sorry," she said, wiping at the tear that coursed down her cheek. "My aunt had received news that her brother had fallen ill. When she arrived in Mulford, Papa, Mama, and Hen… Henrietta were already gone on to their heavenly reward. I had just passed the crisis, but she wanted to carry me away from Mulford immediately. I barely recall the journey to Hertfordshire, but I was assured I traveled with great comfort. Several weeks after recovering some of my strength…I came back…" The words 'to find you' went unsaid. Sophia could not let out that much of the pain she felt.

William faltered into remarkable stillness.

Sophia wetted her lips. "I visited the rectory… just needing to see it once more, and to collect Mother's journals and paintings which had thankfully not been thrown away. I visited Hawthorne Park, and the duchess informed me you had gone abroad." *Without saying goodbye.*

"How long after you left did you come to the house?"

"Less than two months had passed," she whispered.

He flinched, the rage in his eyes growing colder. "I did not leave England until about six months after my father died. And she told me of your passing weeks before my father succumbed to the weakness in his heart."

Sophia gasped, pressing a hand over her mouth.

"I was still here…I must have been in town and my mother…my mother continued her awful deception when you showed up at Hawthorne Park. And we spent almost seven years apart," he murmured, closing his eyes briefly.

"We spent seven years apart."

They stared at each other, and in the tense silence the question lingered.

Now that the truth has been revealed, where do we go from here?

"Why are you here, William?" she did not ask how he came to know her whereabouts, for she had long suspected her aunt would defer to William if he had called upon them in Grosvenor Square.

A soft laugh answered her. A wicked glint appeared in his eyes and then he murmured, "I want *you*."

CHAPTER 5

S ophia's heart pounded a breathless rhythm.
  I want you.

That was the last thing she expected him to say.

"I…I…what do you mean?" surely, he did not expect them to start back where they had left off—with passionate kisses, illicit touches, and a belief they would be married? "You are engaged, and I…I…what do you mean?"

He walked over to her in a slow, predatory prowl. "I am not engaged to Lady Miranda. In truth, she is married to my brother Simon."

"Oh!" oh, why did such sweet relief fill her veins? *My silly, wretched heart.*

The hunger in his eyes stirred an almost painful, sweet ache deep inside her. It was very different from how he had looked at her years ago. Then he'd been a young man of twenty-three on the cusp of experiencing all the vices and sins the world had to offer. His kisses had been passionate, yet sweet and so tender, the memory brought a piercing ache of desire into her heart. Now the man who stared at her appeared worldly...jaded...too experienced and untamed.

William stood there seeming so calm, dripping with traces of water-weed in his hair, his clothes ruined by his wild dive into the swollen river. He was still the same young man she had fallen head over heels in love with but he was older and much altered. His presence seemed too powerful and self-assured for her to feel as relaxed as she used to be in his company. She felt exposed and vulnerable in the need she felt for this man. She had lost so much before; Sophia couldn't bear the thought of letting him get close to her only to lose him again. She would once again be left behind to bear the burden of the agonizing aftermath of losing someone she loved with every breath in her body.

"I'm not the kind of lady you would wish for as a duchess," she said softly. "I never was, despite our youthful foolish attachment, and I daresay I will never be considered suitable with the difference in our circumstances."

His eyes darkened and guardedness settled on his handsome countenance. "I do not believe I mentioned marriage."

The air whooshed from her lungs, and her cheeks burned in alarmed mortification. *A mistress... a lover*. He *had* changed. An odd pain arrowed through her, but also a relief. His pursuit would be one for carnal pleasures only. There would be no expectations she would give up the uninhibited way she lived her life, no fear of his family cutting her, no anxiety that she would never be able to match him in society's eyes because of her lack of connections or wealth. Yet there was a deep pain which lingered, for in the eyes of the man before her she no longer saw love and tenderness, but a dark hunger and a possessive need.

Expelling, a long silent breath, she said, "You wish me to be your mistress?"

His regard was slow and pointedly bold as he perused her body. "My lover...my friend and then we see what the future holds."

The words were said with such carnal intent she trembled.

Fear of feeling too much and to be reduced to

that pitiful person she had been for almost a year rushed through her. "You are outrageous," she whispered, backing up a few steps. "What the future holds? I never wish to marry...*ever*."

A bleakness entered his eyes before his expression cleared. "Then, in the future, we will not discuss marriage."

Her heart jolted painfully at his assurance. "I'll not love you again," she said a bit fretfully.

"Why not?"

"Because when love is lost...the pain...the pain was unbearable. I'll not endure it again. I refuse to!"

"Then I'll not ask you to love me."

A wild fluttering began in the pit of her stomach as she stared at him.

"Meet me halfway," he demanded roughly. "Kiss me, then tell me you do not want me with a similar intensity...that you do not feel hunger to the know the man I am today, and to learn who I could be. Kiss me...and then tell me I am still only your past and I will walk away."

Shock froze her, then a wave of heat seized her, making her tremble. Who was this man, commanding her with such arrogance who expected to be obeyed? And why was she so effortlessly captivated? It was as if her feet had a will of their own as they hurtled her body towards him so that she met him halfway. He gathered her in his arms, dipped his head, and kissed her with ravaging passion. The sensual assault was almost too much, but not enough. Sophia tipped onto her toes and twined her fingers through his hair and held him to her as she responded to his kiss with greedy sighs.

The harsh hunger of his groan settled low in her stomach, hot and urgent. His hands threaded into the length of her hair, and he anchored her to him firmly as he thoroughly explored the recesses of her mouth. For the first time in almost seven years, sensations other than grief or emptiness filled her chest. Yet they were so hard to define, and she could only drown under their intensity. A dark, hot lust slid through her veins, slow and heavy, and she trembled under its intensity. She felt like she wanted to crawl into his skin...his heart...share his pain and give him some of hers. It was as if every pent-up need and anguish that had been bottled up tight inside her for the endless lonely years exploded, and with an over-powering sob she arched into him, her tongue tangling wildly with his.

"How can we start a love affair as if seven years do not lie cruelly between us," she rasped against his mouth, afraid of his answer yet desperately needing it.

His hands were shaking, she realized as he reached out to brush the hair back from her face. "We will take it one day at a time, one kiss at a time."

His low drawl had her meeting his eyes, and she trembled beneath his sensual gaze.

"I am so very different from the girl you once knew."

"So am I. We'll relearn each other…"

"And if we do not like what we discover?"

"We'll walk away," he promised. "This will simply be an affair."

Her heart picked up its rhythm as temptation and unsatisfied desires beat at her. An affair…a taste of passion, a way to ease the terrible loneliness which had encased her heart. And with the boy she had loved and always admired so ardently. So many needs and wants tumbled inside, waging war with the resolve she'd formed to run away from him until she understood the feelings he still roused in her.

He cupped her cheek with his other hand, peppering soft kisses over her lips, then down to her collar. "I missed you so damn much, Sophia," he whispered.

"I missed you too," she said softly. "Even when I hated you for leaving me alone in my despair. I missed you...*ached* for you."

His lips took hers in a sweet, fiery kiss that seduced and ravished her completely, leaving her wanting so much more. Her knees weakened until she could hardly stand as his hand curved around to her bottom, holding her against him while his mouth devoured hers with smoldering sensuality.

Somehow, they made it onto the soft verdant grass, and as they tumbled down, their foreheads knocked together breaking their kiss. Sophia laughed against his lips and when he smiled, her heart trembled at the beauty of it.

"I haven't heard such a lovely sound in years," he murmured, nipping at her throat playfully.

She wore no corset beneath her dress, and she gasped when he deftly unbuttoned the back of her dress and a few tugs later he bared her to his gaze. Her breasts were swollen, rising and falling rapidly, and her nipples were hard. Bending his head, he seized her nipple between his teeth before laving the sensitive flesh with a tormenting tongue tip. The wet heat of his mouth enveloped the tight bud fully, and she cried out in wanton pleasure.

Everything felt out of control...yet so very right.

William eased from her and shed his jacket, waistcoat and shirt. He remained in only his sodden trousers and boots, but she could not remove her gaze from the marvel of his naked chest, still beaded with river water. "Oh William, you are so lovely," she murmured, coasting her hand over his arms and down to his tensed stomach.

He groaned under her touch and closed his eyes as he savored every caress.

Lean muscles rippled and twisted, and his deeply tanned skin appeared as if he had spent a lot of time under the sun without his shirt on!

He rose above her, widened her thighs, and settled between them. His hands brushed against her stomach as he undid the flaps of his breeches. William kissed her lips with soft wicked bites, while he reached down and tugged her dress up high to her thighs. She trembled and whimpers of need escaped her as he bit into her throat…right above her fluttering pulse. He trailed his fingers up the length of her leg. Then he explored farther, letting his hand drift up the sensitive skin of her inner thigh. His diabolical fingers slipped between the juncture of her thighs, parted her drawers.

A wild cry tore from her as William slid one long finger slowly into her wet, aching sex, sending bolts of exquisite sensations through her. Hot, drowning pleasure gripped her as he started a slow glide and retreat. He pressed his leg between hers and shifted his foot widening her more to his intimate caress. Her cry was choked off as his fingers pressed deeper and harder, and she sensed he was preparing her for more.

He kissed her with an almost violent passion, slipped one of his arms under her, gripped her buttocks, caging her into the shelter of his arms with his body. She moaned, returning his kiss with wild abandon as he breached her soft opening with his rigid thickness.

He then thrust deeply parting her unused muscles, which clung too tightly, resisting his possession. Shock buffered Sophia's senses as sensual pain licked at her. He held himself still, kissing her still, distracting her from the pain of his possession. William reached between them with one hand, and she whimpered when he found the nub of pleasure and glided his fingers over it in a rough caress.

She screamed into his mouth at the wicked sensation which arched her more into him, sliding his manhood impossibly deeper. So deep, she lost the ability to breathe. Yet now the throbbing pain had eased, and a sharp, unbridled pleasure remained. She shifted her legs, twining one around his hips and the other around his thigh.

He loved her with such fierce passion and Sophia writhed beneath him, lifting her hips to meet his thrusts. Her cries echoed around in the forest, heating the air with their mutual lust, as her arousal built inside to blistering heat.

She clutched his shoulders helplessly and buried her face in the curve of his neck as he thrust into her clenching core with almost mindless fervor.

"So responsive and sweet," he groaned, snapping his hips even harder.

She clasped his sweat-slicked back and kissed his shoulder too consumed to speak his name, which sat at the tip of her tongue. The sensations rocking through her body were intense, soul-destroying, and then the excruciating pleasure peaked and broke cascading delight through her body.

With a muffled groan and few hard pumps, he withdrew and released on her mound. Sophia blushed fiercely. She could feel the jerking rhythm of his heartbeats against her body. They stayed like that for several moments, until their breathing eased, and her shivering stopped. She watched, fascinated, as his tension slowly eased. William withdrew from her, and she stifled the moan at the sharp ache between her thighs. Sophia's senses felt overwhelmed by his sensual assault. Her lips felt bruised, her breasts tender, and her heart ached. Their coupling had been fierce, passionate, and over too soon.

What now?

She did not look down as he pressed what felt like a silken handkerchief between her thighs, or when he gently tugged her day dress down to her feet. There was more rustling, and then he lowered himself beside her, and she noted he had put on his shirt. He turned his head on the grass and they stared at each other, an inexplicable shyness gripped her in its embrace, and she blushed, then she smiled.

"Will you stay with me at Hawthorne Park for a while."

An unexpected thrill coursed through her. "The duchess—"

"Hawthorne Park is my own," he murmured, brushing a sweat-dampened lock of her hair from her cheek. "My mother is in Bath and I assure you, I will deal with her duplicity."

She could not find it in her heart to think kindly of the duchess, but the ring of icy anger in his tone shot alarm through her. "Please, you must remember that she is your mother…and your Christian duty is to love and honor her. Life is so short and fragile that one day she will depart from the world and you will have to live on knowing you parted on bad terms," she said, familiar grief clutching at her throat.

Knowledge gleamed in his eyes. "Have you forgiven her?"

She closed her eyes. "No."

"Neither have I. But I will bear your kindness and warning in mind when I see her next. I will not chase her to Bath to demand an explanation when you are right here before me. I feel as if I do not want to miss a day without you."

Something hot, yet tender, glowed from his dark blue eyes, and that warm sensation once more unfurled in her stomach. "I am still astonished you are here," she said softly.

He tugged her to his side and curved her into it so that her head was pillowed by his shoulder. "Will you stay with me?"

"For how long?"

"How long does it take to conduct an affair?"

She shifted and tilted her head so she could see his expression, which was one of amused contemplation. "There is a rumor in town that Widow Griffins is Lord Peabody's lover. Not his mistress for he does not provide her with an income or a house or a carriage. And the rumor says they have been lovers for over ten years!"

The eyes that peered down at her were guarded yet watchful. "And you would be content with being my lover for years?"

Her breath hitched. "Could you see to it that I never fall with child?"

His flinch was subtle, but she caught it, and her heart started to pound. "William, I—"

"Say no more, Sophia. I understood all that you said before. I'll not pressure you. And if we are to be friends and lovers for weeks only, or months or years, then we shall be."

She stared at him astonished, her mind mulling over his sincerity. "Thank you, William. I feel wretched and selfish. I had been thinking about an affair...to ease my loneliness but retain my independence. You have now given me that but I can see in your eyes...feel it in your touch that you want *more*...a more I will never be able to give," she confessed achingly.

A decidedly charged tension permeated the air. Would he now say no?

He dragged her up and kissed her with violent tenderness. "I'll take *this*, Sophia. If it is only passion you must give…I'll take it, because anything is better than not having you in my arms."

Relief hit her, and with it, a lifting of spirits. With a sob she curled her hands around his neck, kissing him back with reckless desire. Something elusive whispered through her heart and it felt frightfully like the love she'd clung to for him all these years. It lurked deep inside her chest, sweetness, fire, and fear.

And as William twisted with her so her back was pressed on the grass, Sophia admitted for the first time in years that she had never truly stopped loving him.

Dear God, what am I to do?

CHAPTER 6

Sophia rested her chin on her drawn-up knees and stared at the family's headstone. Leaning in, she brushed a few twigs and leaves from her sister's and arranged the flowers, so they did not hide her name. Aunt Imogen had reburied her family in the family plot so they could be nearby.

"How are you today, Hetty?" Sophia murmured.

A newfound sense of peace settled inside her as she stared at their graves. It had been slowly happening, and with each visit, the pain had grown less and less until an acceptance had settled in her heart. Now when she visited, Sophia allowed only the happiest of memories to cloud her thoughts.

She fancied her family resided in heaven, a place her father had ardently believed existed.

"William is back." Then she proceeded to tell her family about the race with Tommy, the archery competition she had entered with some of his friends who had believed her to be a lad at the time…and finally, she confessed to making love with William.

A blush heated her cheeks as she recalled the passionate way they'd fallen onto the grass and what had come next. After kissing her passionately for several more minutes, he had shown enough restraint when they hadn't made love again. So many emotions had filled Sophia's chest she had asked him for space, and he hadn't hesitated to grant it, only asking her when he should send his carriage for her.

'*Three days*, she'd said. *Send your carriage for me in three days.*'

"He is sending a carriage for me this evening. I…I am going to spend some time with him before I start my travels. I dare not tell Lydia or Aunt Imogen, though I did send a letter this morning informing them I am staying a bit longer in the countryside to avoid the scandal in town. A very good excuse, I believe, and one I am not guilty of saying. What do you think?"

Of course, no one answered, but an unexpected gust of wind rustled through the beech trees, swaying even the heavy branches, and scattering the fallen leaves all over Sophia. She gasped and then laughed. "Is that approval? Or is that you, Papa, screaming your displeasure that I abandoned my virtue without the benefit of marriage?" A thing she still could not believe had happened but would never regret.

Shaking her head at her silliness, she spent another few minutes before pushing to her feet and walking back to the main house. Once inside her chamber, she called for the maid Aunt Imogen had sent down with her.

"I'll be leaving Hertfordshire for a few days," Sophia said as soon as the maid entered.

Mary smiled. "I'll pack for both of us immediately, Miss Sophia. A few day gowns, dinner gowns, a ball gown, and a riding habit?"

"Yes," she said, "but Mary, I shall be going alone."

The maid's eyes widened at the scandalous proposition. "Miss Sophia," she gasped, with evident alarm. "Lady Cadenham bid me—"

"I know what my aunt asked of you," she said with a gentle but firm smile. "I am five and twenty, and I daresay I shall be fine without a chaperone as a guest in a friend's home. I'll accept your company for the journey, but I'll ask the duke for his coachman to return you home immediately."

Servants were notorious for spreading gossip, and Sophia wanted to keep Mary away from spying on her and the duke. The young and excitable maid would not be able to keep whatever she witnessed to herself.

Her eyes widened, and Mary's pale, freckled face was alight with curiosity. "The *duke*? The one in the papers...who chased after you—," said with considerable inquisitiveness.

Sophia arched a brow at her impertinence. Mary flushed and dipped into a quick curtsy before hurrying off to pack. Sophia moved from the escritoire, made her way over to the bed, dipped to her knees, and pulled out a trunk. She opened it and carefully removed one of the nine paintings her mother had done. After carefully wrapping one in several soft linens she bid Mary pack it in her belongings.

Soon Sophia was alone in the drawing room, peering through the windows down the long graveled driveway for the carriage. The book she'd been attempted to read fell, and she picked it up, checking to ensure there was no damage.

She rested her head on the cushions of the sofa, staring into the ceiling. Alone in this drawing room, Sophia suddenly felt like the only person in the world. The yawning emptiness sank into her bones, astonished to realize how often she had endured this state despite the company of dear Lydia, Tommy, and Aunt Imogen.

The roiling emptiness hungered to be filled, and for the first time, she wondered if a mere affair that would be destined to end would be enough to ease the chill of loneliness.

The sound of the carriage pulling into the driveway tugged her attention to the windows once more. Coming up onto her knees and leaning forward, she smiled upon identifying the ducal crest on the equipage. Anticipation and nerves cascaded through her veins, and she took a deep breath to steady the fierce beating of her heart.

She closed her eyes and took a breath through a throat that felt dry and hot. She scrambled from the sofa, stood, and wrapped her arms around herself. The chasm closed, and the icy bite of loneliness abated. The awareness that it was because of

William inexplicably unnerved her yet also filled her with delight.

With a smile, she departed the drawing room toward another wildly exciting experience.

A COUPLE DAYS LATER, Sophia arrived at Hawthorne Park, Hampshire, the ancestral seat of the Duke of Wycliffe and one of the stateliest country homes she'd ever beheld. The grandeur of Hawthorne Park never failed to impress Sophia. The four-story house was perfectly situated atop a hill, overlooking the forest lands and valley that divided the village of Mulford. William had once told her the Tudor-style mansion was built in the late fifteen hundreds, though many modern additions had been carried out on the one hundred and eight room manor. Expansive parklands and impeccably designed gardens surrounded the building, it had the most magnificent sweeping arched entrance and boasted many decorative crenellations and several decorative towers. A few footmen stood in the forecourt of the duke's palatial home and assisted her descent from the carriage.

A footman carried inside two single valises and a hat box, and Mary was sent to the kitchen for food and invited to stay overnight before her return to Hertfordshire. Soon, Sophia stood in the impressive hallway of Hawthorne Park, the air redolent with a mix of waxes and lemon.

"Miss Knightly," the butler said kindly, "Welcome to Hawthorne Park. Please, allow me to escort you to his Grace."

She recognized the butler from her previous visit to Hawthorne Park, but the butler's face was professionally inscrutable. He gave no indication that he remembered the duchess tossing her out before and banning her return. The butler knocked on the door, a muffled voice bid them entry, the door was opened, and she strolled inside.

William glanced away from the open windows at the sound of her approach. A quick flash of primal satisfaction settled on his face, and she realized he'd doubted she would actually come. He took some time just looking at her as she discarded her attractive rose-pink Leghorn bonnet, lined with a deeper rose chiffon, revealing her stunning neatly swept-back hair. Her peach traveling gown had a rose chiffon corsage and a shawl collar trimmed with rose-colored piping. Her beige traveling half-cape was swept off showing the matching rose-colored silk lining and each button was covered with the same silk. She looked a picture and Sophie was delighted she had clearly taken his breath away.

William stood as the door closed behind her, ensconcing them in a silence fraught with intimacy. The duke sauntered over to her, and Sophia trembled as he gathered her into his arms and pressed a soft kiss to her forehead. She closed her eyes, savoring the sensations winding through her. He had a clean, masculine scent that was so rousingly pleasant that she wanted to snuggle closer.

"You came," he said gruffly.

She slipped her arms around his waist and peered up at him. "Doubt me, did you?"

His eyes met hers, and there was something dark and dangerous flickering there. "I have lived in hope these few days."

He lowered his head, and his lips brushed over hers once, so lightly that she barely felt the contact. A sweet feeling flipped several times low in her belly. William stepped away, and she felt bereft at the loss of his closeness.

"I'll ring a maid to escort you to your chambers. You could freshen up and rest a bit before dinner, which has been put back until seven o'clock."

"Thank you, but I would prefer to change and go for a ride. I've been cooped up these last few days, either inside the carriage or a room at an inn."

He arched a brow. "You ride now?"

She smiled widely, remembering how William had tried to instruct her and she failing lamentably. "I do."

Admiration glinted in his eyes. "You've lost your fear of heights? Impressive. There's a story there I am eager to hear."

She lifted one of her shoulders, feeling unaccountably shy. "My mother always wanted her girls to learn to ride. I...I wanted to fulfill her wish."

"I wished I'd been there to teach you," he said, admiration rich in his tone. "I will meet you in the drawing room in thirty minutes for a spot of riding."

"Thirty minutes," she agreed with a smile.

He rang for a servant, and shortly after she was led to a chamber that drew a gasp of admiration from her. The soft plush carpet in swirling patterns of blue and gold perfectly matched the brocade drapes and damask sofa by the fire. The canopied bed in the center of the room had a profusion of pillows, and a lightness filled her heart. William had recalled that she'd told him she liked to sleep surrounded by airy pillows. The maid informed her that there was a sitting room, a separate area for her to use as morning room, and another smaller room for her dressing room. The entire picture was one of elegance and sophistication. Her valises were open, and another maid was cheerily putting her clothes in the armoire.

"And where does that door lead?" Sophia gestured to a four-panel oak door; the only door which was currently closed.

The maids quickly glanced at each other before one answered, "It leads to the duke's chamber, milady."

Heat slowly washed over Sophia's face at the realization that they had adjoining chambers, and that this was not a mere guest room, but the duchess's chamber. What was William thinking? Sophia quickly dressed in her boy trousers and shirt after requesting the maid to assist her with binding her breasts. She laughed aloud, thinking how shocked William would be when he saw her mode of dress. The two maids in the room shared an amused glance, no doubt thinking she had gone off her rocker.

She did not want to hide from the rush of pleasure and anticipation of spending time with William. Instead, she embraced it, humming happily as she allowed her hair to be loose. It tumbled in waves past her pointed elbows and settled near her waist. When the maids left, Sophia twirled in the room, laughing, then she hugged herself.

THE BREATH SEEMED to suck itself from William's lungs when Sophia strolled into the drawing room. The tan trousers clung tightly to her alluring curves, the white shirt fitted snugly, and her hair rippled boldly over her shoulders. An intense jolt of lust hardened his length with such swiftness that for a heartbeat he felt light-headed. She seemed to have discarded to the winds every precept of gentility and propriety. From the exaggerated sway in her walk and the smile of mischief about her lips, William gathered she had meant to shock him.

He was...delighted by this side of her. The girl he remembered had been quite reserved except with her responses to his kisses. He'd thought it because her father was a reverend and he had admired that demure sweetness about her.

Now he felt as if he stared at fire, one which

beckoned him to step closer to its wicked heat. "By God, you look ravishing!"

She made a small and indelicate noise, but her eyes glittered with rich pleasure. He realized suddenly that she was blushing, a delicate pink stain spreading from her cheeks down her throat. She was still not used to artful compliments, *that* aspect had not changed. Waving her to walk ahead of him so he could admire the curve of her derriere unashamedly, they made their way outside and to the stables.

"I can feel your eyes, your Grace," she drawled. "How rude of you."

William grinned. "And where do you feel them?"

She rolled forward even more sensually and he bit his lower lip hard and bit back a snarl. God in heaven. "If you ever dress in such a manner outside of my presence, again…there will be consequences."

"How positively medieval," she said with a light dismissive laugh. "I do believe I shall ignore that audacious command."

An odd possessiveness roared through him, and he loathed the very idea of anyone else enjoying the vivacity with which she glowed. "I'll certainly not hesitate to spank your delightfully rounded arse should I need to impress upon you my seriousness. I'll soothe it with kisses after, of course."

She missed a step as if she'd stubbed a toe and glanced at him over her shoulder. Her mouth lifted at one corner, a wicked little smile. "Oh? I've heard of such perverse pleasures. How *interesting* that you indulge in such pursuits."

It was William's turn to stare as if she had grown horns. The little minx tossed her head and laughed, clearly enjoying rattling his composure. William laughed, and the sound of her giggle as she entered the large stables floated in the air and lodged in his heart.

"Oh, how beautiful they are," she crooned, walking toward two horses chomping at the bit slightly, eager to be let loose.

He'd already sent word for two of his fastest and more powerful horses to be saddled. And now he was glad he'd trusted the instinct that told him she'd want to race, and not want to ride a gentle mare who'd hold her back.

The stable lad's eyes widened when he saw Sophia, and with a nod at the side-saddle, William silently communicated that her horse, a chestnut filly, should be fitted to be ridden astride.

Sophia moved with liquid grace as she eased closer to the horse and with a lift of his fingers, William dismissed the stable hands. Using the mounting block, she seated herself atop the horse with supreme confidence, no hesitation or fear displayed at the sheer size of the beast beneath her.

He walked his horse from the stable out into the yard.

"How long do you wish to ride for?" he asked.

"Until I'm breathless," she said softly, staring at him in a manner that made him want to haul her into his arms and devour her mouth.

He mounted his horse, and in the dimming twilight, they rode out across the rolling lawns of his estate towards the lowering sun.

CHAPTER 7

They rode for almost an hour, at times they raced and other times they cantered admiring the birds they disturbed into flight, the rabbits, and the foxes they spied, and it did not escape William that their conversation was filled with amicable chats of little substance. He still found it pleasant and allowed there would be enough time to find out how the seven years had shaped Sophia and what she truly wished for her future. And for him to see if he truly wanted more than an affair with her.

Everything inside him yelled that a fling would not be enough, but he would proceed with caution instead of hammering with brutal force at her resistance. He did not want to hurt her…that much he knew.

"Let's race toward the skyline of elm trees, where the blue twilight of darkness beckons," she yelled and urged her horse into a run, deeper into the forest abutting his lands.

William chased her, appreciating the exhilaration pumping through his veins, and the power of the stallion beneath him as he easily caught her and passed her. She chortled, brought her horse to a stop, and dismounted with impressive skill. He launched from his horse, and they dropped the reins, allowing the animals to graze and to seek water from a nearby babbling stream.

"Your horsemanship is impressive," he said, moving closer, so they strolled side by side.

"Such a compliment from one as skilled as yourself is a fine thing indeed, your Grace."

He smiled. "What other skills have you learned in the time we've been apart?"

She cast him an amused glance, before bending to pick up a long stick. Gathering another piece, she threw it in his direction, and he deftly caught it. Then she struck an elegant fencing pose.

"*En garde*!" she cried, "*Allez*!" quickly advancing with impeccable style.

Every moment he looked at her, she seemed to offer something new. With a twist of his wrist, he brought his stick up and assumed an offensive position. A delighted laugh issued from her, and she thrust forward in a quick, lithe, and graceful motion. William was impressed and engaged her in a spirited bout of stick fencing.

"I am unable to break through your unwavering guard," she said a bit breathlessly several minutes later, and with thick admiration in her voice. She was breathing hard, flushed, her eyes sparkling.

They continued their dance of thrust and parry, their feet edging forward and back with surety and swiftness over the crunching grass and leaves.

She delivered a straight thrust which he dodged with seamless skill. With another breathless laugh, she admitted defeat.

"Surely not," he said, his eyes crinkling. "I was about to relent from sheer exhaustion. Your energy is boundless, ...and quite enticing." Visions of taking her for hours rolled through him in a dark, hungry tide.

Heat flashed in her eyes, and she lowered her stick.

"I never knew you had an interest in fencing."

In all the long talks they had in the past, she never mentioned the desire. A flash of insight struck.

"Is this another desire your mother had for her girls?"

She smiled, a bit shyly. "No, it was a dream my sister Henrietta had for herself. She pestered Mama and Papa for months, hoping to take fencing lessons. I finally hired a tutor a couple years ago, and then Tommy helped me finesse my form?"

"Tommy?"

"Aunt Imogen's son and my cousin."

"I see."

They came up a tree near to his estate line, a place in the forest where they had met several times in the past. She smiled at him, and with a sigh lowered herself to the thick carpet of grass. He followed, and soon he reposed beside her, staring at the last remnants of the lowering sun in the sky.

"What else have you experienced?" he asked, shifting his hand on the grass to lace with one of hers.

"Oh, this and that," she murmured enigmatically. "Certainly not things a young lady of proper standing would do."

He heard the hidden implication. Not things any duchess would do. "Is that so?"

"Hmm, mmm."

"Tell me," he urged, "What is the wickedest thing you've done."

An unlikely snort came from her. "I sea bathed *in* the water. Shocking, I know."

"Terribly scandalous indeed," he teased.

"Mama always wanted to run into the crashing waters of the sea. We visited Brighton a few summers and the hunger on her face…" Sophia sighed pierced somewhere deep inside of him.

"I always wished we had all donned our sea-bathing suits and rushed towards those frothy waves, and not be transported with a bathing machine!" She chuckled, but it sounded a bit sad to his ears. "I also carriage raced with Tommy. I won," she said smugly. "He was vexed with me for weeks for having bested him since I'm a girl."

"Who wanted to carriage race?"

She turned her head on the grass, and her thick lustrous hair hung in graceful curves over her shoulders, with wisps curling on the softness of her cheeks. "Papa! Can you believe it, William? My father wanted to race carriages with rogues and scoundrels. I suppose as the third son of a baron he had little choice but to choose the clergy as his profession, but he had other desires. How I wished he'd been brave enough to indulge in them, even once!" she ended wistfully.

The touch of moonlight over her face rendered her even more beautiful than William could imagine. He stared at her, his heart breaking for the duality of sadness yet satisfaction he saw in her gaze.

With dawning amazement, he looked at her. "Have you been doing what your family desired to do…these last few years?"

Her lashes briefly swept down across her cheekbones. "It is a fine way to experience life," she said softly with a rather self-conscious smile.

He lightly fingered a loose tendril of hair on her cheek. "You've learned to ride with superb skill, fencing, carriage racing, you frolic in the sea without an ounce of propriety…"

She arched a brow. "Yes?"

"And I suspect a lot more thrilling jaunts."

Pleasure lit her expressive face. "You suspect right," she said with a teasing nudge of her shoulder.

"I also suspect they were all desires your family had in their hearts…and you honor their memory by experiencing it for them," he said gruffly.

She reached out and laced his fingers with her own. "Yes."

"Very admirable and I am glad you found the strength and courage to honor their memory in this way."

Her lips curved in a tremulous smile. "Thank you, William."

He unlaced their fingers, place a finger under her chin, and held her under his stare. "Tell me, Sophia…what have you done for yourself?"

She flinched then froze. Her eyes flared with fiery emotions, and the pain in her gaze hurt somewhere deep inside of him. She tried to withdraw from him, but he did not allow it.

Her gaze searched his for endless moments. "Everything I've done, I've done happily and because I *want* to."

"I know you wanted to…but were they desires of your heart? Things you've always wanted to do?"

Her breath sawed from her throat and fury spit from her eyes, but she answered calmly. "No."

"What do you want for yourself?"

She wrenched from him and scrambled to stand. William followed, grasping her arm and turning her to face him.

"I am heading back to the house," she said without meeting his gaze.

"Such a simple question yet you run."

Her chest heaved as she whipped her head up to glare at him. "I…" she thrust her fingers through her hair. "I survived, William, and they died."

The pain in her voice was a brutal fist to his gut.

"What right do I have to only live the rest of my life by my desires? Those who should be here, Mama, Papa, Hetty…they are all gone! Far too soon before their time and they did not take me with them! I was left to suffer the pain of their passing and how can I do anything less by doing the things they would have done?" she said brokenly.

Unexpected anger whipped through him. "Don't you dare feel guilty for surviving! If there is one thing I know is that your family would never want you to feel less for living when they died."

A pulse became visible in her throat. "How do you know?"

"Because they loved you, Sophia. Your father and mother only wanted the best for you. Hetty was your shadow, and she admired you most ardently and wanted to be like you when she was of age. What you did…living their dreams is beautiful… but you must live for yourself as well."

She slanted him an unreadable glance. "Do not presume to tell me how to live my life!"

He took a deliberate step toward her. "Where is the girl that lay in my arms and dreamed of having three children? The one who dreamed of traveling to France and Italy? The one who dreamed of sneaking into a gambling hall even as she fretted for her eternal soul for having the desire. Where is the girl who dreamed of attending a ball and dancing until her feet hurt? Those were your dreams…and I own they can change, and you might aspire for other hopes. As your lover and your friend, let me tell you, Soph, it is quite fine to dare to dream for yourself."

Wide, wounded eyes stared at him. "I did."

"What?"

She stepped toward him and flushed her body against his. William's pulse jumped in startled arousal at the lush feel of her pressed so intimately against him. She reached up and cupped his jaw before tipping on her toes to kiss the corner of his mouth. Another whisper of a kiss feathered over his jaw, and he closed his eyes against the sensations.

He groaned, stifling the impulse to crush her lips to his. "Soph—"

"By the river, when I allowed you to kiss me, to

enter my body with yours and devastate my senses with such pleasure and passion…" A delicate blush spread through her cheeks. "*That* was me for the first time in years daring to take something for myself."

A breath of need shuddered through him at the memory of how wild and beautiful she had been in his arms. "And I am damn glad, Sophia, that you met me halfway and walked into my arms."

He wrapped his arms around her, bringing her in tighter against his body. Her eyes flared in surprise, but her sigh as she settled against his chest was of contentment.

"I am terribly sorry for your loss, Soph," he said gruffly, dipping his head to press a kiss to her temple. "You lost your family so tragically…and then you believed I abandoned you. I am so damned sorry."

"Pray, do not blame yourself. And while I was lost in grief for several months, I recovered quite nicely," she said with a smile. "My heart no longer cries in the night for them. I found that peace about four years ago. I only think of the fond memories, and I allow myself to miss them without pain."

You did not recover, for you no longer trust your heart to love again.

And he understood. When he'd believed he'd lost her, loving another woman had felt unbearable. And the loss of his father had taken months to fade.

They stood like that, hugging, as the night grew darker, and the forest quieter.

"Thank you, William," she murmured against his chest. Her lips curved into a smile and her fingers dug into the back of his jacket as she clung to him tightly as if she would never let him go.

CHAPTER 8

Sophia had been at the duke's estate now for several days and noted with a mixture of alarm and intrigue that he had made no attempt to seduce her. Beyond a few sweet kisses to her lips, nothing of an intimate nature occurred. His restraint was admirable, for each night, she tossed atop pristine sheets, remembering the way his body had moved inside hers, and the pleasure which had knotted in her stomach and then the exquisite release. William seemed unruffled by their experience, and she was not entirely sure how to feel about that.

They had fallen into a routine that felt domestic, and she was decidedly unsure how to feel about how happy she was at Hawthorne Park with

William. She enjoyed their early morning rides, and then they spent a few hours apart after breaking their fast together. He would retire to his library to discuss estate matters with lawyers and stewards and respond to business correspondence. And she would pen letters to Aunt Imogen and Aunt Lydia, and even Tommy reassuring them of her safety, for Sophia did not delude herself into thinking Mary had kept quiet about her whereabouts.

She had received a letter from Aunt Imogen, which had made her heart pound.

Dearest Sophia,

I am gladdened to hear that you are safe with the duke. You are by no means a young girl anymore, but I do hope you know, the earl and I expect an offer of marriage from the duke after you've been under his roof for several days without a chaperone. I suspected when Wycliffe asked for you that his intentions were honorable, and I plan to hold onto that belief. So, my dear, the decision is in your court, and I know your aversion to the marriage state. I've also allowed you the freedom to leave London because I have never seen you react with such passion to anything in the years since my dear Richard passed, along with his wife and sweet Henrietta. I felt such hope that with Wycliffe once more in your life, you'll start living again, my dear. I urge you to consider his offer with a heart not burdened with worry when he asks you. Society is not aware of your whereabouts, and we must keep it that way. I'll be returning to Hertfordshire in a couple weeks, and I do hope to see you there with us and to hear the explanation of the madness which must have seized your mind to make you travel to the duke's home.

Lovingly, Aunt Imogen.

Sophia carefully folded that letter and slipped it into her valise. Then she opened the letter from Lydia.

Dearest Sophia,

How I miss your delightful company. Society is still agog with whispers of you and the duke, and how they speculate that you are both missing from town! I daresay they are outrageous for they had not thought of you before this! I've attended several balls and made a few friends, Lady Charlotte Simmons and Miss Penelope Mullings. They are quite good-natured and amiable, even if overly inquisitive about your relationship with the duke, who has been labeled the catch of the Season! Of course, I've misdirected them, but I am so positively thrilled that the most eligible catch of the Season has chased you all the way to Hertfordshire. How awfully romantic!

Mama almost fainted when she received word that you are at the duke's country seat. I overheard her speaking with Papa that she fears for your virtue and surely your good senses must have abandoned you somewhere on the road from London to Hertfordshire.

I think it all a grand romantic adventure, and I am quite envious of your position!

Your dearest friend, Lydia.

Slipping that letter in her valise, she stood and made her way downstairs to meet William. He had invited her on a jaunt to the village this afternoon, a departure from their usual activity. At first, she had hesitated, not wanting such an acute reminder of past tragedies, but then a rebellion against her tightly-held fears had sparked inside, and she had relented.

Most afternoons they would picnic by the lake, and take turns reading or regaling each other with bits of their pasts. They dined together nightly, and afterwards they would cocoon in the library playing whist or chess. He touched her at every chance he got and kissed her at least six times each day. She'd counted. But the most delightful part of her stay was the long conversations they had in the nights by the crackling fire as they played chess. Most nights she had fallen asleep on the lush carpet of the library floor, and he would merely lift her in his arms, take her to her chamber and tuck her beneath the warm coverlets.

During their wonderful talks, whenever she questioned him about his years abroad, his answers were terribly vague and noncommittal. Sophie vowed that would change today.

They met in the graveled driveway, and instead of a waiting carriage, two horses were saddled. They exchanged pleasantries and then quickly mounted and trotted away. After riding in the countryside for so long astride, Sophia found her current side-saddle an annoyance, but she had wanted to be properly attired in a riding habit for their visit to the village.

After riding for several minutes in companionable silence, they trotted down the main street of Mulford. The idyllic and quiet picturesque village of Mulford had changed over the years, as evidenced by the new shops which lined the now paved streets, it was clearly a thriving and expanding village. The school had been extended and boasted a larger school yard, a local printer had put down roots and now produced a weekly newspaper for the county, and one of the larger houses now advertised it services as a respectable boarding house. The original village shops had gained a fish monger, and the bakery had taken over the shop next door, which had once been a fairly poky chandlery, and turned it into a small café serving its wares. The bakery was clearly prosperous since the railway had come through Mulford and provided a barrow selling sandwiches and cakes to travelers stopping at the station.

The chandlers had moved down the street to a larger building and now stocked many more items including paraffin for the new paraffin lamps but still stocked the more old-fashioned lamp oil. They still sold the candles, string and other essentials they had previously but now also offered a range of ladies' gloves and some tableware, brought down from the potteries. There was now a post office, and a book shop that also operated as a library.

"Mulford has grown," she said, glancing at him.

"It only needed some investment to bloom."

Sophia admired his patrician profile and astonishing handsomeness. Today he was dressed smartly and as a man of fashion in tan trousers and jacket, a dark blue waistcoat and a white undershirt. His cravat was expertly tied, and a beaver hat settled about his head with an odd sort of elegance. Sophia had donned a yellow riding skirt, with matching half jacket with dozens of buttons leading from midriff to her throat. A narrow-brimmed hat completed her ensemble, and she had perched it at a rakish angle.

"William," she said, dragging him from whatever he had been musing about silently.

A smile edged his lips. "Sophia?"

"Do you have some terrible dark secrets you do not wish me to know?"

Surprise flared in his eyes. "Good God!"

She gave him a swift upward glance, searching his eyes. "You do become very tight-lipped whenever I ask about your experiences during our time apart. Yet you've pried into everything I have done, even getting an admittance that I sneaked a chocolate drink from the kitchen while the household slept!"

His lips twitched. "I've been a bit of a bore, haven't I?" The words carried an unmistakable note of irony.

"You said it," she replied with a laugh.

"I wish I could inform you of grand adventures, but my years were frightfully uninteresting and uninspiring. My father…" he cleared his throat, and his gloved hands tightened on the reins. "My father took ill shortly after cholera reached Mulford. For a while we feared it was that dreaded disease, but that was soon disproved. His heart was failing, and he died a few months later."

"I am very sorry, William, I recalled how much you loved and admired him."

"My father lived a good life, and I have made peace with his passing. My mother grieved terribly, and I too mourned losing you and him. It became unbearable to stay, as I've told you before, and to run from the disquiet I feel I became a bit of a wanderer."

A wanderer. Hetty had always wanted to travel and it had been her greatest hunger. Memories darted through Sophia as images of running from the sweet shop with Hetty, stopping by the milliner to buy laces and fripperies, and on one such run they had caught the butcher's son kissing Miss Amelia Dickson, a very arrogant young lady who had sneered down her elegant nose at Sophia and Hetty. Miss Amelia had always boasted she would marry a lord from Hawthorne Park.

Sophia recalled William's sister observing them from a parked carriage as they had run down this street in the rain laughing like loons. Lucinda— Lucy as she preferred—had been about Hetty's age, had followed him faithfully, and had demanded to meet Sophia. She smiled, recalling William secretly teaching his sister to swim while she had sat on the grassy banks and shouted encouragement.

"How is dear Lucy? I recall her to be so very sweet-tempered, kind, and owning a very romantic disposition for her tender age. Very much how my sister once was," she said wistfully. "How grown Lucy must be now."

He smiled. "I've not seen her since my return to England."

Sophia was for a moment, incredulous. "Surely not! How can you bear it?"

"She is now Countess Riley and is on her honeymoon in Greece."

It felt right that Lucy was already married. The only time she had met Hetty, they had laughed and talked about how grand it would be when they could have fun at balls and dance all night with *beaux*. Lucy had been more confident in her dream, where Hetty had been wistful and had wondered later if as the daughter of a country rector she would ever visit London and take part in the Season's amusements.

"Sophia!"

She glanced around sharply, expecting to see a wildly waving Hetty by the confectionary store with sugar dusting her cheek, her bonnet askew. But the remnants of the memory faded along with the imagined sound of her sister's voice.

"You miss your sister," he said gruffly.

"Everyday. How did you bear being away from your family for so long?"

"It was not easy, but I needed the space to breathe and to live. Only a few weeks after learning of your supposed passing, my mother was callously recommending ladies to me to become my prospective bride and inviting mothers who had daughters she thought suitable to Hawthorne Park. My father also tried to use his continuing illness to force me into marriage, and when I resisted, he asked me to vow that I would not marry below my station."

Sophia flinched and then tried to push past the awful sensation that lodged in her stomach. "You are a duke," she began, appalled that her voice trembled.

"Sophia."

She met his gaze.

"You are my equal in every way that matters."

Her heart trembled perilously, the knot in her stomach untangled, and she could only stare at him in astonishment. There was a tenderness in his eyes that was almost painful to look upon.

"I wrote often," he continued as if he'd not just flustered her. "To my mother, Simon, Lucy, and my middle brother Edward who is in America, but I missed them every day. Edward is to return soon for us to meet his wife. I daresay, Lucy will be home shortly as well, and I shall be very glad to see her."

"I still cannot credit that you insist nothing adventurous happened in your life; you were never the boring sort when you courted me."

He sent her a glance of affront, and she laughed.

"Well, one Miss Phoebe Cranston tried to compromise me into marriage, and I fought a duel in France."

"William!"

There was a twinkle in his eyes. "Shall I leave those recollections for later when we repose by the fire?"

"You would not dare. I thought you were in India all this time. However did you end up in France!"

"Each place I visited was spent in the pursuit of pleasures and anything to distract me from your loss."

"You…you've had other lovers," she said, her eyes widening.

Dark eyes slashed to her. "I thought you dead. And even then, it still took me years before…before a woman interested me in that manner."

"I do not judge you for it, nor does it make me uncomfortable." But she did have the awful thought she might not have measured up to his exotic experiences be the reason why he'd made no attempt to ravish her again.

She narrowed her eyes on him, and his eyes widened in mock alarm.

"Sweet mercy, what are you *thinking* about?"

"I wondered if you found me boring compared to…" she waved a hand, unable to voice the sudden doubt which had burned through her. "Your other women which is why…since that day…"

A shocked gaze collided with hers.

She looked away, suddenly made uncomfortable.

"No, you will look me in the eyes."

The command was laced with steel, and she snapped her head up. Her gaze clashed with the savage brilliance of his. It was then she realized their horses had stopped in the middle of the street. Thankfully only one parked carriage was about, and it was some distance away.

Her heart was suddenly suffused with an ache. "William, I—"

"You will listen to me and listen well."

Sophia felt her heart begin to beat a little harder. "Yes," she whispered. "I'm listening."

He nodded once, tightly. "Do not ever compare yourself again to women and situations I do not even recall. You were all I thought about when we were parted. I grieved for the loss of your sweet presence. You are all I think about…all I dream about. That day by the river, you damned near killed me with your sweet, wanton responses. You will always be the most desirable woman to me, Sophia. Do not ever doubt it again."

A startling warmth invaded her, and the shock sent prickles all over her body. It wasn't a declaration of love, that would have scared her, but his sincerity pierced that cold, lonely place that had existed deep within her for so long and filled her with a burst of heat. Tears burned her eyes and throat. She blinked them away, dashing her hand across her eyes.

"I'll not," she whispered.

The hard edges of his mouth softened into a pleased smile. "Good."

They continued, and he showed her the new

sewage system that had been placed in Mulford after the tragedy years past. It was then she noticed with some astonishment how cleaner and crisper the air felt, that several buildings in the town had been painted and refurbished, and as she toured with him, she realized it had all been his doing.

"How have you accomplished so much in Mulford?"

"I started before I left England. And though I was away, I continued my work through letters. I trusted the stewards I left in charge."

A few people in the village had looked at her with shock and alarm, and Sophia nodded politely to those who had known her and her family.

"They too thought I had died," she said faintly, at the buzz of interest that followed her and the avid stares and whispers behind fans.

"Yes," he said gruffly, bringing their horses to a halt in front of a memorial.

He dismounted and then assisted her down from her horse, and with a gasp, she walked over to the exquisitely craved standing marble piece, her heart shaking when she spied her name along with eighteen others.

"When I returned to Mulford…I only went to the rectory," she murmured, tracing her name. "A new rector had not been appointed, and the place was empty. The key still rested underneath a flowerpot. The gardens my mother tended so lovingly had been choked with weeds, and many flowers had withered. There was an air of desolation about our empty cottage. I did not stay long. I could not bear it. I collected a few belongings which had been boxed, and just left there. I could have taken my aunt's carriage to your home, but I needed to walk through the forest, to smell the heather on the air and the moss and the oak. To hear the animals as they scuttle in the bushes. I trekked to Hawthorne Park, and in that long walk, for the first time in weeks, I found a measure of peace."

She glanced up at him. "I was so devastated by your mother's dismissal and your leaving that when I returned to the carriage, I insisted on leaving Mulford immediately. The journey had been difficult…I remembered when I returned to my aunt, I took to my bed for several days. I had never returned to Mulford until now."

He drew her closer to him. "I'll have it corrected immediately."

She stared at the memorial for a long time, memorizing the names and recalling the faces of those she had been friendly with. Sophia bowed her head in a silent prayer for a minute, then turned away and allowed the duke to help her remount.

As they rode back toward Hawthorne Park, her heart felt unburdened, empty of any pain or grief, and she smiled, a peaceful sort of happiness blossoming through her. She sent him a sideways glance.

"Thank you for taking me with you today."

THAT NIGHT, Sophia stared at the connecting door, leading to the duke's chamber. She tossed restlessly, unable to sleep. Huffing a breath, she scrambled from the bed and went for her valise. She opened it and removed the painting of her mother's that she had wrapped. It wasn't large, and she'd had it framed. Taking a deep breath, she padded to the connecting door and opened it without knocking.

William stood by his window in a dark blue silk banyan, a drink in his hand. Her feet sank into the plush oriental carpet, and she saw the slight tightening of his elegant fingers around the glass. Sophia smiled and paused by the foot of his large canopied bed in the center of his room.

He faced her, and a flash of hunger lit in his

eyes before he masked his reaction. She wore a loose short-sleeved night rail, the neckline cut low enough to show a hint of her unbound breasts. Sophia admitted she had wanted to see that burn of desire in his gaze and had deliberately not tugged on a robe. Her heart stumbled in her chest before continuing with a more frantic beat. She curled her bare toes into the carpet. "I wanted you to have this," she said huskily.

He made his way over to her and took the offered painting.

"By God, this is exquisite!"

"My mother painted it," she said softly.

"This is of my father when he was a much younger man."

"Mama said she met him once when she and Papa called upon Hawthorne Park at the duchess's invitation. Mama said he had been so compellingly handsome to her, that she went home and had to render his image against the backdrop of the night stars and the forest. I…I thought you should have it."

"Thank you," he said huskily, drawing her forward and pressing a kiss to her forehead.

They stayed like that for a minute, where she closed her eyes and simply basked in being so close to him. She stepped back and smiled. "Sleep well, William."

His dark gaze watched her as she turned and walked away from him.

"Stay with me for the night, Sophia."

He arrested her retreat with that firm command. She spun around, his eyes collided with hers, and he held her gaze for a long, timeless moment. He rested his glass on a small table before the chaise longue and led her to the bed.

They slipped beneath the covers, Sophia turned to her side, and the duke curved behind her and slipped his arms around her. His hardness pressed against her thighs, and she felt when his manhood flexed. A shiver of want darted through her body, and her core ached. She wiggled experimentally, and a harsh groan slipped from him, but he made no move to seduce her.

They stayed like that, and she snuggled back further into his arms, loving that she was surrounded completely by his warm, masculine form. She felt safe...cherished, and with a soft exhalation, she relaxed and allowed her eyes to drift closed. "This is where I want to be," she murmured.

"And here is where I want you."

"Why are you not seducing me?"

She felt his smile on her hair.

"I'm waiting," came his rejoinder.

"On me to pounce on you?" she asked, teasingly and quite sleepily.

Yet something warned her it was not that, even if she were to face him now, fling one of her legs across his hip and nip at his throat he would show restraint.

"What are you waiting for?"

He made no answer, and as she drifted into a deep slumber, she heard a low murmur at her ears, "For you to fall in love with me, my darling, Sophia."

CHAPTER 9

The last two weeks had been an exercise in torture, not in restraint. As William stared down at Sophia in his bed, with a feeling of such contentment he had never known before filling his heart. Last night with her softness curved into his body, he had slept deeply without disturbance for the first time in several days. His nights had been restless as Sophia had stolen his ability to sleep. He wanted her by his side forever, he admitted ruefully, a thing he doubted she would want to hear. In her eyes, as they peeked at him occasionally, he saw an aching need but at other times he discerned wariness. As if she was afraid that she was falling too much back under his spell.

He drew aside the dark silver and blue tasseled

drapes letting in the bright sunlight into the room. She muttered some choice word under her breath, and twisted away from the light, grabbing the pillow and slapping it over her head. Delight filled him. His Sophia was not a morning person, and the sheer nightgown had ridden up high on her thighs and bared one of her luscious cheeks to his gaze.

His mouth dried as his cock jerked in anticipation of being inside her again. William studied the elegant curves of her hips, which were sensually flared, and the rounded globes of her buttocks that made him want to lower his teeth and bite that firm flesh. He sat on the edge of the bed and could not resist the urge to touch her…just once. He smoothed his hand over her back, relishing the feel of her delicate curves, the feeling of rightness.

She purred and breathed his name on a whisper of a sigh.

What if she never falls in love with me again? A painful, aching tightness lingered inside of William and a cold knot began forming in his gut. Despite the wicked temptation of Sophia, and the invitation to make love which glowed in her eyes with more heat daily, he had been waiting to see that softness in her eyes, that shining aching love before he took her to his bed again. Once he saw it there, he would make an offer of marriage and pray that love would be stronger than the fear of eventual loss.

He could not keep her at Hawthorne Park forever, not with the considerable risk he'd already placed her reputation in. Nor would he set her up as a mistress. Never would he truly dishonor her in such a manner. If she did not come to him soon, with more than fire and passion, he would urge her to return to her aunt and then try his hand publicly at courting her.

She would possibly run from him if it came to that, but he dismissed it. The Sophia he knew and the woman before him now were so courageous and not afraid to face life. The fact that she had flourished when so many hardships had been stacked against her was a testament to her strength. A feeling of loss suddenly tore through him. He should have been there over the years to see her stunning growth into the charming, bold, and impetuous woman she was now.

You'll make a fine duchess and the best of wives, he silently praised her.

He pressed a kiss to her shoulder and left her to sleep. It was still early yet, but he had business to attend to. One of the cotton factories he'd invested in was on the cusp of shutting down, and another housing venture had run into problems. There was also the matter of the recent investments he had made in the London Stock exchange, and another of his estates in Cornwall which needed modern mining and farming equipment.

Reluctantly he made his way from the room to his library to meet with his steward and one of his solicitors. His meetings were intense and moved slowly for the day, and he blamed it on his fractured thoughts.

Sophia distracted him to the point that his man of affairs threw him several glances, and after only two hours, he conceded defeat and rescheduled his meetings for the following week. The thought of eventually relinquishing her if she refused to come to him left a bitter taste of regret in his mouth and a dark pain in his heart. He needed to step up his game and start a more ruthless campaign against her heart.

A FEW DAYS had passed since Sophia had awakened in William's bed feeling peacefully contented, when he announced he had a wish to fulfill. She had thought he desired to give her something in return for the painting she'd given him. Sophia had hurriedly assured him that reciprocation was not needed, and the dratted man had only given her a mysterious smile.

Following his instructions, they had traveled to London discreetly where they had booked into Brown's Hotel in Mayfair. Of course, she was suitably disguised in trousers which fitted her frame perfectly, an evening jacket, a white shirt, and a silver waistcoat. To her delight he had even procured her a short dark blonde wig, and fake spectacles which were perched on her nose. Sophia did not believe she looked like a man at all, but society seemed content with the disguise for no one had paid her any particular notice each time that she had walked through the hotel lobby.

The carriage rumbled through Mayfair, and Sophia tapped her feet on the floor of the equipage barely able to contain her excitement despite not knowing exactly where they were heading. She bit into the soft flesh of her lips to prevent herself from asking William about their destination for the third time. The man was very tightlipped, and she had to admire his single-mindedness.

She brushed aside the carriage curtain and

peeked out into the darkened streets. They trotted past townhouses and a few parked carriages, but nothing she saw indicated where they were going. "William…"

He grunted, and she grinned. She launched from her seat and landed in his lap with all the grace of an elephant.

Oomph, he groaned, looking pained.

She slipped her hand around his neck. "William, my darling," she began to cajole.

"I'll not tell you," he replied, amused at her eagerness. "I see the mischief in the twinkle of your eyes and the curve of your lips. Let me inform you, Miss Knightly, no threat can loosen my tongue, no kisses or soft touches can entice me."

She fisted her fingers through the thick strands of his hair and melded her mouth to his in a very soft but persuasive kiss. "Not even one like this?"

"I am made of stern stuff," he said, returning her brief kiss before leaning back with a scowl.

"You are heartless!" she murmured, nipping his chin. With a sigh, she went back to sit facing him, folding her arms beneath her breasts and glaring at him.

The dratted man winked, folded his arms across

his chest, and leaned back his head against the squabs as if he would go to sleep.

Sophia smiled, a piercing tenderness swelling inside her chest. William had arranged a surprise for her. Suddenly it did not matter what it was, only that she would treasure it. She got up, sat beside him and leaned her head on his shoulder. He relaxed with a sigh of contentment as if he had been waiting on her.

Oh, William…how I wish I were braver.

For the last few nights, she had slept in his arms, and despite their snuggled proximity, he hadn't seduced her. Sophia found that she relished the comfort of being in his arms, and she found herself yesterday wondering what it would be like to stay with him always.

I could be his duchess. Of course, it was a role she did not think herself suited for, but Sophia was also confident in her abilities to learn and adapt. As his duchess, she would be expected to throw lavish balls, dinners and house parties, and even support several charities. Her stomach tightened, and her heart started to pound a little bit faster. She closed her eyes and imagined being with him each night, laughing and playing chess by the fire, riding across the lanes of their estate, waltzing at balls, having a child together.

And what if I should gain such a joy and then lose it. An iciness closed around her heart. The ache in her chest became a physical thing. Her heart fluttered madly, and her chest rose and fell with her uneven breaths. The pain and fear that crowded her senses felt like a physical assault. She snapped her eyes open and bit once more into her bottom lip.

As if he sensed her disquiet, William shifted, placed his hand around her back and shoulders and clasped her to his side in a closer embrace.

Death is a natural passage of life, she reminded herself silently, banishing the anxiety.

"You've gone quiet." His voice held a note of contemplation.

"I'm thinking," she murmured.

The carriage rumbled to a halt, and she sat up straighter against the squabs. "Oh, William, where are we?"

The sliver of moonlight glinted off the sharp angles of his cheekbones, and he flashed a sensual smile. "Now, Sophia. I promise you, there is absolutely no chance of you going to hell once you've step foot in this establishment, but it is very important to maintain your disguise as a young man."

She stared at him, blankly. Going to hell? Then she gasped, quite dramatically. "You are taking me to a gambling den!"

"Yes."

She spluttered. "I was a foolish eighteen-year-old girl when I mentioned *that to you*. A piece had been printed in the newspaper about their lavish decadence and vices, and I just thought maybe... maybe I could glimpse inside one." She clasped her cheeks and groaned. "I should not have told you!"

"We could always go back," the devil offered.

She quickly rallied. "And let all your hard work go to waste? That would be such a shame."

He grinned. "I hope you recall how little convincing I actually had to do."

They climbed out of the carriage, and she glanced around the fog-shrouded night. It was late. Almost midnight. Her body felt incredibly alive, every sense feeling somehow sharper. They strolled toward the large door, and Sophia was fairly hopping with excitement. She ignored William as he rolled his eyes at her undisguised glee. The door swung open without his knocking, and then they stepped into sin and decadence.

The decor was lavish, sinful, and a place she should be refusing to go for fear of her immortal soul. Her father had pounded out many sermons on the ruinous nature of these type of clubs. Sophia looked around as if in a daze. She felt oddly off-balance and doubts that she should be in such a wicked place settled in her heart.

"You are safe with me, always."

The words washed over her senses, and inexplicably all the anxiety that had started to stir inside vanished. The interior was one of such lavish luxury, red and green carpets covered the floor, and swaths of red and golden drapes twined themselves around massive white Corinthian columns. Dozens of tables were scattered in an organized sprawl on this lower floor, and many lords and revealingly dressed ladies sat around the tables cradling drinks in their hands, some with cigars in their mouths.

Several lords and ladies tipped their glasses to William upon his entrance, but only dealt her a dismissive glance. Of course, she was not a duke, so there was no need to fawn over her. She barely suppressed the urge to roll her eyes.

Smoke wafted through the air from the many lit cigars, glasses clinked loudly as it appeared every gentleman had a drink in hand, and the clattering of dice echoed as they rolled on the tables. She watched, impressed, as young men dressed in black and white elegant evening wear shuffled, flicked, and cut cards with artistic expertise. Elegantly clad women with filigree masks on their faces, and a fortune in jewelry at their throats and ears reposed on chaises longues chatting and drinking champagne.

"Welcome to The Club, a gambling den owned by Viscount Worsley."

As if William had instructed her, she glanced up at a balcony at least three stories up to see a man leaning on the balustrade overlooking his domain like a dark king.

"I've read about him in the scandal sheets," she said. "They say he is wicked and unprincipled, a wolf in lord's clothing."

"It said all that, did it?" William drawled with provoking amusement.

"I swear upon my honor, those were the exact words."

"Do you wish an introduction?"

She lifted her face to his. There was such an air of wickedness and debauchery at this club and a pulse of forbidden desire arrowed through her heart. "No…I want to play cards, faro, Macao, whist, and vingt-et-un…and drink brandy."

Her lover arched a brow, and a wicked glint entered his eyes. "There is a room here solely dedicated to prizefighting matches."

Sophia laughed at the sheer audacity of it all. "Here? How truly *wicked* of him. Isn't that illegal?" Then she gasped, "I had read in the news sheets some time ago of a lady of society being revealed here. That she…fought someone in the ring?"

"I've heard of this as well. I believe that the lady is Countess Maschelly."

Sophia stared at him. "You jest!"

William laughed and tugged her through the scandalous crowd. The revelry and raucousness was startling and astonishing. A wicked, daring thrill pulsed through her as she stopped at many tables watching and learning. When her duke pressed a glass of brandy between her hands, she almost kissed him. She had leaned on her toes and then caught sight of his fierce scowl.

Giggling, she had moved away from him, shocked that she had forgotten she was disguised as a young gentleman.

About an hour later, he took her up some winding stairs to the first level to a door that led to a fight. A man stood by a large oak door. He bowed slightly, pushed open the massive door, and they stepped into another opulently fashioned room with soft dark green carpets cushioning their steps. The lights in this room were dimmer, the tables less raucous. Sophia felt a queer sense of vulnerability when they entered the fighting den. She gently fixed her spectacles which had slipped down her nose.

"Would you like to place a bet?"

"I would win money if this person wins?"

"Most assuredly."

She thought on her inheritance her father had left her, and the desire to travel to France, Italy, and Versailles. And also, the knowledge that she could not live with her aunt forever, though she had been invited to. "Yes."

William led her to a table and then went and placed their bet on the man he believed could win.

"How much did you place?" she asked, rubbing her hands in anticipation.

"One hundred pounds."

She squawked at the exorbitant sum. "And if the man should lose?"

He sent her an amused glance. "Then I've lost one hundred pounds."

"I've lost it. I mean to pay you back whether I

win or not. You've only advanced me the bet," she said fretfully. "It is no wonder men lose fortunes in these places."

Footmen darted adroitly between the tables delivering drinks, and she took another glass of brandy, already warm from the previous drink. A large roped area in the center of the prodigious room was the only place well lit. Soon two men approached the ropes, dipped under, and made way to the center of the ring.

"Oh dear," she muttered, scandalized. Both men were stripped to the waist, their chests and torsos on alarming display. The men wrapped thin leather strips that had been soaked in water or perhaps vinegar around their hands.

Their names were announced, the fight started, and Sophia sat straight in her chair, riveted by the brutal dance and parry. Jarring slaps and thuds as fists met flesh echoed in the room. "This is barbaric," she breathed, truly shocked at the brutal display.

It did not last long before one of the men dropped onto the floor with a resounding thud. Several people cheered and clapped.

"Congratulations, my dear, you've won one thousand pounds."

Sophia twisted to face him. "Dear God, are you certain?"

"Quite."

"Oh!" she threw her arms around his neck and kissed him quickly on the lips. She giggled at his softly muttered curse. "Relax, if anyone saw you, it will only be said you are a man of varied and exotic tastes."

His mouth came down on hers, fleeting but hard and passionate. The subtle hint of brandy flavored her tongue, and she moaned in delight at his fierceness and unexpected sensual assault.

She felt breathless…and hungry.

"What do you want to do next? Lord Huntley keeps a masquerade ball tonight. I received an invitation."

"As long as we can go somewhere to kiss endlessly."

His eyes darkened. "We can do that here."

"Oh, let's," she purred against his lips.

Without speaking with anyone, they stood, and he tugged her through the throng and exited the fighting den. They traversed the hallway and then came upon a silent and dark staircase.

"You have private apartments here?"

"Yes."

"And we are going there now?"

"Yes."

They clambered upstairs until they reached the landing. In the silence of the corridor, at a large oak door, he paused and fished keys from his pocket, and opened the door. She was ushered inside, and she halted in the center of the room. It was richly decorated in swaths of green and black. A chaise longue that appeared specially built was flush against a wall, near a fire. A small table with a decanter with amble liquid stood in the center of the room.

The door closed with a decisive *snick*, and she spun to face him. The air crackled with the intensity of his stare. He cupped her cheeks between his large hands, bent his head, and crushed her mouth beneath his own.

She touched him with a featherlight caress, fleeting and tentative, gliding her fingertip across his jaw.

"Be daring with me, William. I've so missed the feel of your body pressing deep into mine."

"Ah my sweet, I've been very mindful of your sensibilities."

A delicious shock ran through her. She lifted her eyes to his, and the heat in his gaze strangled her breathing. "I know…we are conducting a very odd affair if I dare to say so. I've been under your roof for over two weeks, and not once have you commanded me to your bed for ravishment."

A dark sensuality settled on his face, and a shiver went through her.

"Lie down on that sofa there," he ordered, lifting his glass toward the dark blue damask sofa by the roaring fire.

Shock scattered Sophia's thoughts as she stared at her duke. "William?"

"If you please, take off your trousers and undergarments, so your pretty pink quim is bare to me."

CHAPTER 10

"Leave the shirt on. You'll place your feet on the edges of the sofa and open your legs wide."

Heat swept through her in a violent wave. A startled laugh escaped before she choked back the sound. "William…I…" She blushed at the picture of what he wanted lodged in her mind. It was scandalous!

"Do you need liquid courage?" he drawled, holding up a glass of what appeared to be brandy.

"I do not need spirits to be daring," she said, lifting her chin, but the fingers that loosened the waist of her trousers trembled. Her hands fell away and she took a few steady breaths. To be so bare and vulnerable before him. The shirt was just about long enough to cover her bare bottom, but once she opened her legs like he'd commanded, he would see *everything*.

He leaned against the edge of the large desk, his face washed with carnal intent. "Afraid?" he asked with provoking amusement.

She narrowed her eyes. "Never.... merely wondering if I should order you to strip as well."

Appreciation lit in his brilliant eyes, and his soft laugh brushed against her skin like temptation itself. Lifting her chin, Sophia removed her boots and stockings, stripped from the trousers, and knee-length drawers. She shrugged from the jacket and dropped it to the floor and removed the waistcoat. Only the shirt remained, and its edges brushed over her bottom like a lover's caress.

"Remove the spectacles...and the wig."

She complied and even took it a step further, drawing several pins from her hair until her tresses tumbled in loose waves down to her back. Sophia sat on the sofa and gripped the edges as an inexplicable shyness almost overwhelmed her.

Her lover's smile faded a little, growing softer, more intimate. The deep blue of his eyes glinted with wicked knowledge, and he prowled over to her. William lowered to his haunches and peered up at her. He encircled her left ankle and pushed up until her knee bent, so she sat with her leg drawn up, the sole of her foot flat on the edge of the cushion. Her breath hitched when he leaned across, his beautiful eyes holding her captive, and repeated the action with her other leg. Her entire body blushed when his gaze dropped to her revealed sex.

"So lush, pink…and already wet for me."

A queer excitement rippled through her stomach. She expected him to touch her there, but he did not. He shifted, resting on his knees before her. He leaned in, and the touch of his tongue on the back of her knees was as light as butterfly wings. Tension tightened low in her belly, and her pulse raced. He went higher with his light kisses, and Sophia gasped at the wickedness of it.

"William?" she moaned, desire and uncertainty pulsing inside her.

He nipped along the insides of her thighs, then applied the tender ministrations of his lips. Then he was there, at her open sex, with his wicked tongue, which slid through the tender folds of her quim with erotic precision.

He slid his hand underneath her bottom, gripped, and pulled her even closer to the edge of the well-padded sofa. Her breath came in shuddering gasps, and a sob rose in her throat when he licked her again. He held her legs wide, bent and licked in one heated swipe before drawing her nub of pleasure into his mouth and sucking hard. She screamed and slapped a hand over her mouth.

He showed her no mercy. Sophia gripped his hair, her weight dropping back against the plushness of the sofa. Nothing should ever feel this good but also so agonizing. "William, please!" she wailed.

She sobbed his name, undulated her hips, whispers and hoarse cries ripping from her throat, and he never released her from under the lash of his tongue. The exquisite sensations built steadily, overwhelming her senses.

He came over her and roughly ran his lips to her neck, where he bit hard. A jerk of her shirt and buttons burst away. He nuzzled her collarbone and then lower capturing her nipple with his mouth.

Trailing his hands down, he cupped her neglected breasts, which felt so heavy and swollen with desire. He rolled her nipples between his fingers, pinching and pleasuring her. Desperate to have him in her, she pressed her hand between them and reached for the flap of his trousers. Soon his thick hardness rested in her palm, and she gripped him tightly.

He groaned in ecstasy.

He held her gaze as he entered her slowly. Her breath caught at the tight, stretching sensation as he pushed deep inside her until he could go no deeper.

"I love you, so damn much, Soph," he said his voice dark with desire.

Words of love hovered on her lips, and the realization they were there struck fear in her heart, and she shivered in the cage of his arms.

"No," he said, taking her mouth in a raw domineering kiss. One that seared her insides with molten heat. "Stay with me. I do not want these doubts in your eyes, my darling, only feel what is between us."

He withdrew, so that only the tip of his manhood nudged her entrance, and then plunged deep. Her hoarse scream slid over them. For an instant, they both lay unmoving, then he dipped his head and pressed the softest of kisses at the corner of her lips. A deep ache of want and complex needs filled her soul.

"I love you," he murmured again, awe in his voice as if he held a treasure in his arms. A very strange but sweet twisting ache stirred in her belly, and her heart quickened.

His voice caressed her like a physical touch, soft, smoky, soothing, sensual.

"Love me, William," she pleaded, kissing the wildly pounding pulse at his throat. "Take away the doubts I feel rising in my heart." She hated the doubt that still lingered and she wanted to remove the shadows in his eyes. He mattered to her so much.

He started to move with savage sensuality within her, and she cried out, glorying in the pleasure-pain that spread through her tender core with each snap of his hips. He snaked a hand below her stomach and pinched her clitoris between his fingers. For endless minutes, Sophia became lost entirely in the taste, the scent, and the feel of him. Wonderful shocks of sensations speared her senses, and she orgasmed in an exquisite burst, shaking and gasping. He rode her through her convulsions of pleasure, and soon he found his release deep within her body.

He eased from her and shifted so that she sat atop him. She wilted onto his chest, relaxing into the haven of his embrace, her body still shivering through the aftermath of such untamed loving.

IT HAD BEEN three days since William had returned with Sophia to Hawthorne Park. There was a heaviness inside his chest, for each night, he confessed his love after they had pleasured each other, and instead of love growing in her eyes, they were shadowed by doubts and fear.

They lay in the drawing room on a chaise longue by the fire, and she was only clothed in a billowing white shirt which hung to her knees.

"William," she began hesitantly, and ice congealed in his stomach.

"Yes?"

"I…I cannot keep staying here. I must return to Hertfordshire. My aunt is traveling down in a few days, and I will need to be there to greet her."

Silence blackened the room. He had known he could not keep her there forever without marriage.

"I'll miss you," she said in the fraught silence.

"Do you plan to never see me again?" He chided. "I thought you said affairs lasted for years."

Relief bent her shoulders, and she twisted atop

his chest. The ice deepened. This was what she wanted—an affirmation their affair would continue further not the tender sentiments he had been bestowing each night. The hollowness in his heart spread, and his hands tightened on her shoulders.

"William?"

"I understand you must go," he said gruffly.

There was an odd sheen of tears in her gaze as she stared at him. "I've been thinking about wintering in France this year."

Another harsh blow to his chest. "I see."

"Would you...would you come with me?"

The air whooshed from him audibly. "As your lover?"

She smiled shyly. "Yes, I am a thousand pounds richer, and I've heard the French are less judgmental of *affaires de coeur*. No one there would know we are not man and wife." She lowered her eyes as her cheeks pinkened. He could feel the beat of her heart against his chest. His Sophia was anxious.

The door swung open without the courtesy of a knock and anger snapped through him. Who would dare!

He snapped his head up to see his mother frozen in the doorway, her face a mask of astonishment and anger. William eased a blushing Sofia from his chest. "I am certain the butler told you we were not to be disturbed," he said icily.

"So, it is true," she accused, stepping further into the room and slamming the door closed behind her. "I saw a shocking damning piece in a scandal sheet in Bath! My good friend Lady Palfrey asked me who is this Miss Knightly that you would chase her and create a spectacle of yourself. How dare you bring this…this woman to Hawthorne Park and betray everything your father—"

"Silence!"

His mother flinched as if the raw anger in his voice had flayed her skin.

Her hands fluttered to her throat, and she had the temerity to stare at him with wounded eyes. He turned to Sophia who had lifted her chin in defiance, even if her cheeks were stained red with her mortification. Her lips were swollen, and her hair mussed, quite revealing evidence as to what they had been doing earlier. "If you will but grant me a few minutes with my mother."

She stood on wobbly legs, bent and tugged on the scattered trousers. They had raced across the estate a few hours ago, and when the soft misting rain had started, they had returned to the drawing room to play chess but had been distracted by their passion. Sophia nodded regally, spun about, and made her way from the room without acknowledging the duchess.

"What rudeness!" his mother snapped. "But that is to be expected from someone so lowborn and vulgar and willing to act the whore."

William turned and stared at the woman he had once loved with his entire heart. He'd always know her to be kind and thoughtful of others, but that seemed to only extend to those of similar affluence and blue blood. "You will never speak another crude word about Miss Knightly ever again," he incised with chilling authority. "You *lied* to me."

No shame glowed in her eyes. "And I do not regret it," she said firmly. "Or you would have foolishly married that—"

"I hope one day I will be able to forgive your despicable actions! I am ashamed of you, deeply!"

She paled and swayed alarmingly, but he did not rush over to her.

He moved closer to her, uncaring of his state of disarray. "I never imagined my mother…the woman who kissed my knees when I scraped them, who first taught me about love and kindness could hold such contempt and prejudice in her heart. You told me she was dead." All the agony he'd endured crowded his throat, and his breath hitched audibly. "I mourned her," he said gruffly. "I screamed for days…months, and when the pain was unrelenting, whisky became my companion. And you knew she lived."

Tears slipped down her cheeks, but he was not moved by this evidence of some regret. "I believed her to be a passing fancy. Nothing more."

"And does that justify your wicked deceit."

"William—"

"Miss Knightly is the woman I love with every part of me."

"And does she love you?" she began scathingly. "Or does she love your wealth, your influence, money and—"

"She loves *me*," he said with quiet force. "And hardly gives a damn I am a duke."

His mother lips parted, and her eyes glowed with shock. "You asked her to marry you?" she asked in a bare whisper. "You promised your father—"

"How dare you try to control me through a man who is dead!" he snarled, anger throbbing through him in riotous waves. "My father is *dead*, and I will not be bound by his prejudices, nor will I allow you to have a say in the woman I take to be my wife. I love you, Mother, but you will respect my wishes without interference for I will not hesitate to walk away from you."

"William!"

"You will leave Hawthorne Park and only return upon my invitation. And Mother...that might never be."

She swayed, pressing a hand to her chest as if unable to move. Concern bit through him, but he swallowed it down, refusing to be manipulated by her. She had cost him so much with her wretched desire to select his wife.

As he made his way to leave, his mother flushed her back against the door and splayed her arms wide.

"I'll not hesitate to lift you and drop you on your fundament outside!"

Sophia was determined to leave him, and William was at a loss as how to convince her to look past her fear and choose him. But he had to try and had no time to waste on his mother's theatrics. William feared she was not ready to choose him now, but he would not chase her to France. If he gave in now and kept pretending only an affair would do, nothing would ever be good between them in the future. He'd already laid a farcical foundation by not courting her, but stupidly taking her to be his mistress.

No more. She needed to risk a gamble, and he prayed it would be on him.

CHAPTER 11

Sophia hurriedly dressed in her most serviceable gown and walking boots. Temper simmered in her veins at the duchess's rudeness, and she was also angry with herself for feeling mortification at being found undressed in William's arms. Fixing a hat atop her tightly bound hair, she made her way down the stairs.

"You told me you were seeking a wife...a duchess," his mother's voice echoed through the thick oak paneling of the door.

Sophia faltered, a hand lifting to her mouth. William was seeking a bride. Why did the notion hurt and frighten her so much? His response must have been calm and measured, for she did not hear him, but a shrill rebuttal came from the duchess,

"You cannot mean to marry that social climbing upstart!"

Anger whipped through Sophia, and before she could think it through, she wrenched open the door to the drawing room and spilled inside. William's face was cast in cold anger and discomfort traveled through her heart to see it.

"William, I recalled you told me your mother was ill with a malaise. And please bear in mind what I told you about losing your loved ones when least expected. While it is not her business, and she does not deserve an explanation, I believe it will greatly relieve her stress and very likely collapse if you inform her of the truth about us?" she said, ignoring the duchess for she truly did not care for her and would not deign to give her a scrap of her attention.

Silence fell, and miraculously even the duchess seemed to have lost her tongue.

"My intention this year was to take a wife. It was one of the reasons I was at Lord Huntley's ball. To dip my toe in the marriage mart. I do intend to marry. Not to anyone but *you*."

The duchess swayed, and Sophia stared at him helplessly. Those softly spoken words had lodged themselves deep inside of her. Her heart started to pound as the awareness that this really was not a simple affair for him scythed through her. "I...I...I cannot marry you," she whispered, her voice breaking. "I only wanted a discreet affair, that is all."

Her heart squeezed at the admission and the hunger that had been beating inside for more quivered.

The duchess did not seem capable of deciding on what she wanted, for now she carried the expression of one deeply affronted. "*You*...you dare to deny my son...a duke?"

Sophia exhaled, twining her own hands together, squeezing hard. "I told you at the beginning, William. This...whatever we have can only be temporary...only an affair. It is the only reason I came here."

"I know," he said, and in his eyes, she spied something tender...and patient.

"I will not love you!" she cried. "I'll not risk my heart to such pain ever again. Don't you dare expect it of me, William? Don't you dare!"

"Sophia...you already love me."

The soft, confident words were a brutal blow to her chest, and she stumbled back, staring at him. She bit down on her cheek, dragging in a hard breath, resisting the tears that threatened to overwhelm her. "Thank you for these last couple of weeks. I'll treasure them forever. But I have nothing more to give."

She turned to walk away, and he said, "Sophia...wait," arresting her movements.

Her heart pounded, her hand on the doorknob, she turned her head and met his stare.

"I fell in love with you the first time I saw you playing in the forest with a puppy chasing you. When I was told you died...I died too. I tried to drown away thoughts of you and how deeply I loved you in liquor, vice, and work. Nothing changed. Everything inside became hollow and empty. I resolved to take a wife and fulfill my obligation to the title, but I never cared whether I would ever be able to love that mythical lady...for I had nothing more to give. Until I realized you were alive. Everything that had been painted in grey and coated in ashes and bleakness was suddenly filled with color and purpose. For you my heart beats gladly...with you my soul is happy. I too despair of the day I might lose you...but those intervening years Sophia...they can be filled with happy memories...memories that will keep us going through life if we were to ever lose each other. It is better to live our love than deny it because of fear," he said hoarsely, laying his heart bare to her in a manner she had never imagined he would.

He took a step forward. His eyes contained a flash of challenge that stole her breath. "Will you meet me in the middle, my love?"

Her heart was a slow thud inside, and she imagined loving him with every emotion in her heart and losing him. Her knees trembled, and she leaned her side into the door. The pain of it was too much to even think of such a situation. "No...I...I cannot, William."

He flinched. It was so subtle, but she caught it, and her heart broke even more.

A gasp sounded, and Sophia's gaze switched to the duchess. The duchess had a hand over her lips as her gaze volleyed between them, an unexpected awareness dawning in her eyes.

Acting on the instinct of flight, Sophia wrenched open the door and rushed outside. She hurried toward the butler.

"Sir, I am leaving Hawthorne Park immediately. Please have my belongings packed and delivered to Countess Cadenham's home in Hertfordshire."

Surprise widened his eyes. "Should I call

around the carriage for you, Miss Knightly," the butler intoned gravely.

No, that would take minutes she could not spare. Minutes where William might drag her upstairs and…she closed her eyes, shutting off her wild imaginings. What she needed to escape was the fear and panic clawing at her throat.

"No, I'll be fine." There was a path which led from his estate to Mulford. It might take her hours to walk it, but she would make it there and possibly impose upon Squire Blagrove to loan her his carriage to take her home.

Sophia rushed forward, and the butler opened the door. She made her way to the eastern side of the estate and started on the track that would lead her to the forest and then to Mulford.

She did not want his love, for surely, he would want the same thing from her. And giving him any more of her heart would lead to such agonizing pain should she ever lose him. And what of children? Sophia stumbled, pressing her hand to her stomach. Children. Hunger roared through her with such fierceness she trembled and started to cry.

But I could lose them too…

"I'll not love you, William Astor!" she snapped

as she walked even faster, almost stumbling in her haste. "I'll not marry you!"

Losing his support, his tender love following on the deaths of her family had twisted something inside of her, but it hadn't fully shattered. But now as she hurried down the dirt-beaten path away from Hawthorne Park and his mother and her condemnation, Sophia realized with each step, it was as if a knife sliced into her belly and twisted.

The love which had shown in his eyes just now, the joy which she had felt the last several days with him. Not once had she thought of death or pain or the fear of loss. There had only been time for living, for enjoying each other, and she knew a lifetime with William, each day would be a revelation, a blessing, a joy they would treasure.

Her steps slowed.

Something huge and powerful swelled inside of her, a revelation she could not shy away from. If she kept walking, she would never see him again, or touch him, or hear his voice, or see his smiles, or feel the bliss of him making love with her. Everything would go back to how it was before she had seen him at the ball. A life of fun with rollicking jaunts, but with no genuine contentment with her lot in life. And the very idea broke her.

Wild, unimaginable grief filled Sophia's heart, and she cried out. She wanted to be with William. They had only been together a little over two weeks, and Sophia knew she loved the man even deeper than she'd loved the boy. He made her yearn to live…hunger to claim all the dreams she once had in her heart. And only with him.

She spun around and started running back the way she came. Endless seconds passed, and she did not stop, desperate to reach him, hating the pain that he must be feeling that she had run from him after he laid his heart open to her. A sob hitched in her throat, and she panted harshly, but she did not stop. Holding the folds of her skirt, Sophia ran and ran. She saw him in the distance, hurrying down the path she had taken.

He'd chased her. And at that moment, she realized he would always come for her even when she did not see clearly and ran from her fears.

Oh God, William, she cried silently, too winded to speak.

He hurried down the path, his face cast in anguish. When he saw her, he faltered, his expression becoming guarded even as his gaze wandered over her as he clearly tried to decipher

her intention. She barreled toward him as fast as she could and hurtled herself into his arms, knocking him back a few paces. He did not hesitate, wrapping his arms around her and squeezing her tightly. She heard the long, slow breath of relief he blew out.

Sophia thrust her fingers through his hair, and pulled his head down, crashing her mouth onto his. He made a faint noise of surprise but returned her kiss even more fiercely.

"Forgive me for being so stupid," she said against his mouth, her own lips trembling.

"I am certain I will. Maybe tomorrow, for you gave me a terrible fright."

"I love you!" she cried. "I never stopped loving you, William and I cannot bear the thought of not having you with me, always. Forgive me." She pressed kisses all over his jaw and lips. "Forgive me, William!"

He was hers, and she was not letting him go.

Abruptly his arm was beneath her knees; he was scooping her up, lifting her. She buried her face in the crook of his neck.

"Where are you taking me?"

"To my chamber, where I plan to make love to you until you are too sated to stir."

"There is a bit of way to walk, William," she said on a choked laugh. "And your mother—"

"Do not mention her to me. I've not let her off lightly. I've banished her to the dower house and have cut off her allowance. Nor will I invite her to our wedding. She does not deserve to bear witness to our day. One day I am certain to forgive her, for I love her, but it will not be for some time, nor will she enter our home until she has apologized sincerely to you…and you've forgiven her."

"I am so sorry," she said, hugging his neck even tighter, hoping to soothe the pain she could still hear in his voice.

They reached the main entrance, and the butler opened the door, his face stoic as if he saw his master every day chasing a lady and bringing her back to the house in his arms. He walked past his mother who rushed out of the drawing room as if she'd awaited his return to speak with him.

A scandalized gasp escaped her when she saw them. But William hugged Sophia even tighter to him and shifted to face the butler. "My mother is to be escorted from the premises and all her belongings sent to the dower cottage in Brighton. She is not permitted entry in this house or on the grounds of Hawthorne Park unless my duchess decrees it, and if there are any doubts about her identity, she is in my arms."

Mortification mottled the duchess's face, but she kept her lips firmly sealed.

William walked away with her, and at the base of the stairs, he said to the staring butler, housekeeper, and maid, "We are not to be disturbed, and dinner should be sent up on trays. And for breakfast and luncheon tomorrow." Another pause where he thought about it. "And perhaps another dinner tray. We will, however, require a bath to be set up in the morning."

Sophia giggled at the servants' expression of scandalized titillation.

Her love started climbing the stairs. "Are they still there?" he huffed.

She peeked over his shoulder. "Yes. Even your mother. They are staring up at us with varying degrees of shock and amusement."

"Impertinent!" He groaned. "I am about to drop with you, but I dare not put you down if they are watching. The rumor that would reach as far as London townhouses would not be flattering to me."

She pealed with laughter as he huffed with each step he took to up the stairs.

"There it is," he murmured, pressing a kiss to her forehead. "The sweetest sound I've ever heard."

At the landing, he peered down at her, and she realized he was not winded at all. That act had been solely for her…to make her laugh. "I do not deserve you."

"Wrong, you deserve the world to be laid at your feet."

"I love you so, William."

"So, you'll be my duchess then?" he asked as he deftly opened the door to his ducal chamber.

"And your friend…and lover… I'll love you in this lifetime and the next," she said on a softly shuddered breath, her eyes glistening with tears.

A powerful need flared in his eyes, and he bent his head to brush his mouth along her temple then down to her lips, which he claimed in a deep kiss. He tumbled her onto the bed and proceed to ravish her with exquisite thoroughness for the night, and long into the next day.

THE EPILOGUE

Dearest William and Sophia,

I have held onto my foolish, obstinate pride for over a year, and I must confess I am deeply regretful of the hurt my actions caused you, William and Sophia. I've tried to justify my actions by saying I wanted the best life for you with a lady of quality, reputation, and connection. For so very long I believe those were the perfect attributes my children needed in their life partners, and that belief persuaded me to act in the most villainous manner.

I dearly hope you will forgive me, William. I was not at your wedding, and it grieved me. How my heart shattered to read of the news of my grandson's birth announced in the newspapers.

I would like to attend his christening, and perhaps have tea with you and your duchess, if she will have me,

*and I daresay I hope with my full heart to atone for my
actions.*

Your loving mother, Amelia, the Duchess of Wycliffe.

S ophia lowered the letter and folded it carefully.
Her husband reposed under a large elm tree
by the lake, their four-month-old son, Alexander,
snuggled into the crook of his arm sleeping.

They had exhausted him with play, and even in
sleep, his cherubic countenance wore an expression
of satisfied delight. Feeling William's eyes upon her,
she shifted her gaze to see her duke staring at her.

"We can do no less than open our hearts to your
mother since she graciously apologizes and asks for
forgiveness," she said, leaning over to brush a kiss to
his lips, careful not to wake their child.

His eyes shadowed, and she understood. With
how happy they had been, the notion that years had
been lost to them because of a wicked deception
was often painful to accept. But the joy they found
in each other this past year was more than Sophia
ever dreamed possible. Her happiness was a living
entity within her heart, and she found there was no
time to fear when they might be taken from her, or

she might leave them. Each moment and each day were revelations of joy that consumed their hearts.

"I will respond to my mother and invite her to Hawthorne Park."

"And I shall welcome her...and perhaps we can see about mending the hurt."

His eyes smiled first, then his lips curved. "Thank you, my Sophia."

William carefully shifted, coming up on his elbow and placing their son in his padded cradle. Once their son was secured, she curved herself into his arms with a sigh of delighted contentment. A sensation, rich, sweet, and vibrant coursed through her. "I love you so, William."

He melded their lips together in a kiss which quickly flamed into passion. Always it would be this way with them, fierce and burning with love, yet also sweet and tender. With a sigh and a soft moan, she sank against him. "I'll not be ravished in front of my son," she teased, sliding her hands around her neck.

He kissed the tip of her nose. "I love you, Sophia. In this life and the next."

In this life and the next. A loving possibility Sophia believed with all her heart.

THANK you for reading **Sophia and the Duke**!

I hope you enjoyed the journey to happy ever after for William & Sophia. REVIEWS ARE GOLD TO AUTHORS, for they are a very important part of reaching readers, and I do hope you will consider leaving an honest review on Amazon adding to my rainbow. It does not have to be lengthy, a simple sentence or two will do. Just know that I will appreciate your efforts sincerely.

ACKNOWLEDGMENTS

I thank God every day for my family, friends, and writing. A special thank you to my husband. I love you so hard! You encourage me to dream and are always steadfast in your incredible support. You read all my drafts, offer such fantastic insight and encouragement. Thank you for designing my fabulous cover! Thank you for reminding me I am a warrior when I wanted to give up on so many things.

Thank you, Giselle Marks for being so wonderful and supportive always. You are a great critique partner and friend.

Readers, thank you for giving me a chance and reading my book! I hope you enjoyed and would consider leaving a review. Thank you!

ABOUT STACY

USA Today Bestselling author Stacy Reid writes sensual Historical and Paranormal Romances and is the published author of over twenty books. Her debut novella The Duke's Shotgun Wedding was a 2015 HOLT Award of Merit recipient in the Romance Novella category, and her bestselling Wedded by Scandal series is recommended as Top picks at Night Owl Reviews, Fresh Fiction Reviews, and The Romance Reviews.

Stacy lives a lot in the worlds she creates and actively speaks to her characters (aloud). She has a warrior way "Never give up on dreams!" When she's not writing, Stacy spends a copious amount of time binge-watching series like The Walking Dead, Altered Carbon, Rise of the Phoenixes, Ten Miles of Peach Blosson, and playing video games with her love. She also has a weakness for ice cream and will have it as her main course.

Stacy is represented by Jill Marsal at Marsal Lyon Literary Agency.

She is always happy to hear from readers and would love to connect with you via my Website, Facebook, and Twitter. To be the first to hear about her new releases, get cover reveals, and excerpts you won't find anywhere else, sign up for her newsletter, or join her over at Historical Hellions, her fan group!

Printed by Amazon Italia Logistica S.r.l.
Torrazza Piemonte (TO), Italy

16716816R00116